VALERIE HOLMES

MADDIE MULLIGAN

Complete and Unabridged

LINFORD
Leicester

First published in Great Britain in 2018

First Linford Edition
published 2018

A catalogue record for this book is available
from the British Library.

ISBN 978–1–4448–3874–9

Published by
F. A. Thorpe (Publishing)
Anstey, Leicestershire

Set by Words & Graphics Ltd.
Anstey, Leicestershire
Printed and bound in Great Britain by
T. J. International Ltd., Padstow, Cornwall

This book is printed on acid-free paper

MADDIE MULLIGAN

Desperate to leave a life of poverty and ill treatment behind her, Mairead Mulligan agrees to marry Samuel Blackman, a man she has never met, and leave Ireland for the Settlement Straits of Malaya. On the way to Dublin, she has the good luck to fall under the protection of Connor Riley, a mysterious man of means, and the two are drawn to each other. Suddenly, a new life across the world with Mr Blackman holds little appeal — and Mairead must make some difficult choices . . .

1

'Maddie Mulligan, have you lost what little sense that head of yours possessed? You cannot just walk out on your family on a whim! What on earth do you think you're doing? How are you going to live? Get back in that kitchen and hang up your coat; you're going nowhere.' Ma's words echoed in my head, but I knew I had to do something. If I stayed, I would bring shame on my family, and that I could never do. No matter how detached from them I felt, I would not bring the wrath of the church down upon their heads. Shame carried a tarnishing stain on all those associated with it. Ireland was a beautiful land that I would always miss, but it had strict rules and expectations. I was a misfit — I never could settle to it. My pa would never forgive me, even if Ma managed to, eventually. I was twenty-two and my life needed to be my own.

'Ma, I cannot. I must leave now. I'll write. You would never understand . . .' I saw her eyes flash, she was about to lose her rag with me, but what was new? When had she the patience of the saints when it came to her eldest?

'Wouldn't I? Have you given me a chance? You are behaving like an eejit.' She shook her head and wiped her fingers on the front of her apron, wringing its folds between the troubled, shaking hands. 'How will we know you are well? What do we do when we need you? Who'll look after young Jack, Bobbie and Braden?' She sighed heavily as she drew new breath.

Finally, I had the truth of it. The shaking of hands, the waving of fingers was nought about my leaving, but about her having to do more work caring for her ever growing brood.

'Peggy or Biddy, perhaps?' I offered up the names of my siblings, looking directly at her. I was challenging my

2

mother — unheard of and disrespectful, but far too long overdue. This woman who feigned affection and pride for me whenever I'd done well with my schooling, pleased the nuns — a difficult fate to achieve at the best of times — or been given an extra stamp at Sunday school, or simply did an acknowledged kindly turn for the neighbours, then I was her pride and joy. Behind the proverbial closed door, the rest of my life was dogged by her incessant nagging and complaints. It grieved me to say or even think it, but she was no mother that I wanted or needed. God forgive me for thinking it, or to ever become one such myself. I did not want to be a mother who spat insults at her daughter day after each tedious and predictable day. I just wanted to be free.

'You know that cannot be. Young Peggy's going to be the bright one, and our Biddy is already walking out with Joseph Kelly, and your pa's — '

'Working until he stops at the pub for

a jug, spending money he can ill afford, and then he'll come home to his dinner that I'll have prepared, looking at his children with admiration because they'll have clean hands and faces that I'll have washed, whilst you'll take his coat and hat and the credit for all I've done, Ma.' I took in a breath as much to calm my nerves as well as my temper. This row had been a long time brewing, but never could I say such in my father's hearing.

She folded her arms across her apron-covered bust. For a moment my eyes watered up. All I had craved for years was an ounce of respect or a hint of love. 'Why can you not see what you do? Why can't you think on me as you do Peggy — your 'pearl'?'

She cut across me, my plea unheard as usual. 'You should have been on the stage. You are a sour miss if ever there was one. The green eye is what you have. You're jealous of your sweet sisters.'

I chose to ignore her latest put-down. 'Young Peggy is only two years younger than me, Ma. She's no so bright as crafty, I'll give you that. So let her peel the spuds, wash her siblings and go on errands. Biddy, not a year younger than me, has had two dates, chaperoned by his elder sister, so that is not exactly a courtship, Ma. You need to stop talking to old Nancy O'Brien and do some work yourself. This is the 1930s, not the 1830s!'

'Holy Mary mother of our beloved Lord! You have a mouth on you that would shame the saints, Mairead Mullen!' Her whole head was going a strange colour, beyond a blush. I wondered if I was selfishly bringing about her end, or was it just that she had more than her usual dander up?

Calmly, I placed my small bag down in the hallway. It held little enough. Looking at it on the door mat, I sighed whilst I pulled my old coat straight, tilted my hat over my long dark hair and then wrapped the knitted brown scarf around my neck, before tugging on my matching gloves. They had been knitted from the unravelled jumper of one of her pa's castoffs and had little give or flexibility in them, but they managed to keep my hands moderately warm. 'Waste not, want not' was one of Ma's favourite sayings, unless it came to Peggy wanting something, Biddy walking out with a Kelly, or some coin for the boys' needs.

I watched her predictable next move as she blocked the doorway. 'You ungrateful little wretch! I knew you had a spiteful heart, Maddie Mullen, but if you go out there with nought but what you're wearing on your back, and well, to put it bluntly, lass, that is where you'll end up — making a living on it.' Ma's finger prodded my shoulder, but despite the harsh words I did not step backwards.

My heart felt stabbed as the truth of Ma's resentment for me was finally revealed.

'Is that it? Are you . . . have you?' Ma's eyes lowered, resting her vision on my stomach.

'Spiteful, is it? That is what all my

hard work has been thought of. You think I'd do that?' I picked up my bag. 'I'll not have you demean yourself any more, Ma. You talk like a woman from the docks sometimes. I just want to leave. Please move.' I stared at her, swallowing back a sudden wave of emotion as the enormity of what I was casually doing hit home. Praying to whatever charitable god would listen, Catholic or Protestant, whichever truly ruled o'er us, that He would allow me to have joy and love in my life and not turn Ma's cruel words into a harsh reality. I'd rather die than live a life like that. I would not see my family again, not for a long time. I might resent my parents' favouritism of my siblings, but the boys were only children and I would miss them all. But I knew that if I stayed I would be used until all of them had grown and no beau would look at me, tired and worn down by life and toil — left to die an old maid; spending my life in the shadows, a burden, and dependent on my brothers' charity, an embarrassment to all. It was a dismal thought that I could not abide.

Why could the woman who stood in front of me, lips set in a stern line, eyes cold, never look at me the same way she did my younger brothers or sisters? Instead, I was ordered about or coldly ignored.

'It takes money to live, you stupid eejit. How are you going to survive? You'll be back here in no time. What will Father Ryan think if he hears that you've run off, your reputation in ruins? The shame of it!' Her fists were now balled.

'Ma, if I stay there will be more shame, for I aim to marry and you would never allow it. So I'm going, and that is that!'

Ma's eyes widened unnaturally. 'What do you mean — marry? Who would have you? How did you meet a man? When have you had the time, and where have you been?' Her glances at my stomach continued as if it would suddenly grow before her eyes and my ultimate sin be betrayed. Such faith she had in me!

The look of total bemusement on Ma's face almost made me laugh out loud. I was telling her something so shocking that she could not take it on, and yet she had missed any sign of it. Something serious had happened under her nose and she'd had not a sniff of a rumour. She and Nancy O Brien, the gossip of all Ireland, had missed it too. Even in this closed community, none had realised that Maddie Mulligan had been making plans for a whole year.

Of course, I'd not actually met the man yet, but it had all been arranged. I had a good education with the nuns and knew my letters well. I read the papers in the village shop and Pa's when he brought one in. I had seen my Samuel's small advertisement for a companion wanted for a long and exciting journey to a new life in the Straits. He had not expected a woman to respond. Boldly, I had. We'd shared so much information about each other and our dreams that it was obviously a joining of mutual souls. Destiny had played its hand, and he insisted that marriage would be essential, and so we would commit body and soul to our future. The feeling that swept through me as I thought on those words — that commitment — filled me with such warmth. To have someone of my own to love and be loved by, my Samuel. For nearly a year I'd shared my thoughts and dreams, and he had told me about his previous journeys.

I always collected the post from the shop, never waiting for it to be delivered home. No one wrote to anyone there anyway. Samuel and I shared the same desires. We were going to have a new life in the East — neither Liverpool nor Newcastle, but the real East, the Far East. Together we were going to the Straits Settlements of Malaysia. Mr Samuel Blackman was already an assistant on a rubber plantation near the capital city of Kuala Lumpur, and I would soon be Mrs S. Blackman. It would be a life far removed from this that I could envisage and Ma could never even dream of. She was afeared of even taking a trip to Dublin.

Ma's anger caused her bosom to heave as she waited for me to explain, but I just shook my head. I had to go now, or it would be too late. 'I'll write, Ma,' I promised, but stepped quickly back as the door was pushed open.

The tall frame of my very sober pa blocked my way. The heavy wool of his coat and flat cap was covered in moisture from the thickening mist.

'Oh Patrick, you've no idea what the lass is saying . . . ' Ma blurted out her drama-filled words. Her voice was never so harsh when she spoke to Pa or shouted at us in front of him.

My heart sank as I realised something was going terribly wrong with my plan. He should not be here. He was staring at me as if his eyes would pin me to the living-room wall.

'Yes, I do, Bridget. And you don't take on so now. The lass is going nowhere fast, unless it is upstairs with me belt behind her backside.' He glared at me as if he knew all. But how could he? I'd been so careful.

'Pa, you don't know what you're saying. You've been drinking. I'm . . . I'm old enough to know me own mind! Let me pass. I will write and explain when you've had time to calm.' I had come this far. I had to be strong and bold and stand my ground.

The door slammed behind him as he pushed it with a fist. My body jerked involuntarily as the heavy clasp locked shut.

'You are bringing no shame to me, lass, not in my lifetime.'

'No more than she already has,' Ma spat out her words, but looked down as Pa's glare momentarily shot to her. He put a hand in his pocket and pulled out a letter, waving it in front of me like a flag that signalled the end of a race.

I recognised Samuel's writing straight away. 'What are you doing with this?' I put my hand out to take it from him, but he held it away from me. I did not want to step closer to him. I feared he would grab me and did not know what he would do. He was icily calm, and I felt the chill. I knew his temper was bad; worse when sober, as then there was no excuse for it. He knew fine well what he had done and why when the darkness overcame him.

'Father Ryan picked it up from the post and gave it to me for safekeeping. The man is turning blind eyes to your shame for my sake, but you've been writing to an Englishman for how long? Did yer think no one would know? The Father knows all. He hears confessions and the troubles and worries of idle tongues who love to stir the murky peat of the bog. You bloody eejit. I took you to have more sense.' He sighed heavily, and I saw a nerve at the corner of his left eye twitch, something I'd never witnessed before.

My heart felt as though it had missed a beat. Hetty O' Reilly at the shop had suspected something and told the priest!

He stormed past me and into the living room, where a fire still burned low in the grate. I could not grasp my beloved Samuel's letter before it fell into the flames. I went to snatch it back, but Pa grabbed my arms and held them to my sides as I watched it burn, its secrets forever beyond my reach. I sobbed, but held back the full outpouring of tears. No, I'd not cry, not in front of them. They had broken my heart, spoiled my plans, but I would not let them break my spirit . . . not anymore.

'Ma, put her bag in the kitchen. She can unpack it when we let her out,' Pa commanded. He was not shouting but speaking low, unusually so. It made me swallow involuntarily as I faced him. Guilt gnawed at me as he looked proud and yet crushed. I had not wanted to be here when they found I had gone. It was better to make a clean break, I'd thought. The word 'coward' came to mind.

'What do you mean, let me out?' Temper fuelled by fear made my words sound as desperate as I felt.

'Exactly what I said. When a dog acts badly, yer beat it and leave it in the doghouse. I don't trust meself to beat you at the moment, so that's to come; but you are going nowhere!' He grabbed my right hand and yanked me after him. I tried to pull away but he spun around to face me.

'Don't even try if you value the skin on your back, lass!'

I did not pull away again. I'd never seen such rage in him. He marched me to the outhouse.

'No — you can't! I need to catch the — '

'You'll not be catching anything bar a cold and whacking when I've time to take the thought of murder from my heart. You sit and count yer blessings and ask the good Lord for some more come morning — for you, lass, will, need them. You'll be here for two days and nights at least; and when you next see light of day, you'll spend the rest of the year trying to make up for your selfish sins. A daughter of mine running off, and with an English! Never! The only straits you are going to live in, Maddie, are the desperate ones you have created for yourself.' He put his hands between my shoulder blades and pushed. I was hurled bodily into the darkness of the stone lockup we called the outhouse. I crashed into a bucket and fell, spread-eagled on the floor. Sitting up, I glared at the sliver of light that managed to break the cold unmitigated gloom I had been left in.

Damn them! I had eight hours left to catch the train. My ticket and money were on me. Bag or no, I could still make it . . . if only . . . I could escape!

2

I had no idea how much time had gone past; it may have only been minutes, or it could have been more than an hour, but I hammered on the old door to no avail. Being ignored was as hard to take as being shouted at — worse in fact, because here there was no way to reason with them. I hoped they had not sent for the priest.

A movement in the corner of the building made me hug myself tightly. I hated mice and rats, and had no idea which was in here with me. I did not want to stand in the dark, so I moved into the sliver of light. I had to think calmly.

They had discovered my plan because I was a naive little fool who had no understanding of how far people's curiosity and gossip delved into their neighbours' lives. Why not let people live their own lives and follow their own destiny? I knew the answer too well. Because theirs was so predictable, controlled and planned out for them, lest death, illness, war or famine changed it.

Shaking my head and wringing my aching fists out, I felt the full weight of guilt and sin on my shoulders. Yet to stay here now was to give my life up to raising my siblings in never-ending shame with little hope of redemption. Had I betrayed their trust, the love of the boys? None of it was their fault. It was Ma's!

I hammered and hammered at the door, frustration building with each painful blow. No one had even bothered to shout me down to silence the racket I was making. So I tried looking for a tool — anything to pick the lock or loosen the hinge, even something to lever it. I would not give in! Time and tide waited for no man, or woman, and I had my majority now. I would not be treated as a helpless child.

The sound of approaching footsteps

was as a figment of my imagination, breaking through my thoughts. Was it Pa's? I heard hobnail boots on the old stones of the yard. No! They were lighter and the knock on the door far gentler as someone rapped against it and began turning the key in the lock. Bracing myself, I waited as the door creaked open. With a straight back and determined head held high, I waited to face whoever had returned to me.

In a split second of fear, I stepped back, ready to make a bolt for it if it was Pa with his strap. His temper was short and quick when it took over him. It was with more than a little relief that I realised the form taking shape in front of me did not even half-fill the doorway — it was slight and also shivering from cold or fear.

'Peggy!' I whispered. Never had I been so pleased to see my sibling who I fought with nearly every day of my life in some snappy exchange before Ma told us, or rather me, to silence my tongue. 'Have you been sent for me?'

She stared at me silently for a moment.

'Let me slip away . . . please?' That final word resonated with me — I did not usually ask for favours.

'No, they don't know I'm here. I . . . I . . . heard that you tried to get away . . . to run off with an Englishman!' She glanced back at the house.

I was surprised at the bitter edge there was in her words. 'Yes, I have to. I am dying here. Peggy, understand, please. I was going to write to you once I was safely at my destination and explain.' Suddenly my words felt shallow even to my ears. Selfish perhaps would be a better description, and I felt worse because all I still wanted to do was leave.

'I do. I want you to go too!' The quiet words hung in the cold air between us.

I felt their stab as I realised she sincerely meant them. They were not spoken out of defence or bitterness of the moment, but were wholeheartedly meant.

20

'Peggy, I — '

'You're not one of us. I don't know the hows or the whys of it, Maddie, but you've not an ounce of Pa's blood in you, I'm sure of it. Every day you're here, your dark hair seems to stand out against our auburn. I'm sure he knows too, but loves Ma too much to say ought and risk shaming her more than your presence here does. So before his boys are old enough to look at you and wonder why your appearance is so, just go and leave us in peace.' She shrugged her shoulders as if that was all there was to her words; a dismissal.

I took a step back from her and gasped. I could not believe that what the girl was implying could be true. If it was so apparent to everyone else, why had I never thought of it? Everyone knew that to have a father other than your named one was a sin God would never forgive. Yet there was a stark truth being spoken here that echoed inside me.

'Why risk his wrath for me, Peggy?' I

edged nearer the door jamb and pushed gently past her lest she suddenly think better of her actions, and with great relief stepped outside into the cold air.

'Here.' She held out a scorched letter — my Samuel's, rescued from the flames. 'He tells you where to meet him.' In her other hand she had my bag.

'Thank you!' I grabbed the letter and hugged her tightly, but she froze with her arms straight by her sides.

'I'll have none of that,' she whispered in my ear. 'You were leaving with bad blood in you and you're thinking only of yourself. Go. I want nothing to do with you; don't write me, for I'll not read your words. Leave us and stay away from my family. You're making a big mistake, but then bad blood will out; you might find you like the life at the dockside. That's where he'll leave you once he's had his way. Ma said so.' She turned on her heel.

'Peggy . . . ' My word was just loud enough for her to hear. She paused, but did not look back. 'You don't believe those evil words, do you?' I asked.

'Aye, I do.' She locked the door to the outhouse. I did not move for a moment.

'How will you explain my escape?'

'I won't. When Pa sobers up, he'll think the faeries let you go.' She shrugged. 'Let him.'

She stormed off back to the house and I collected the bag she had dumped on the floor by my feet. I would not cry — I would not!

Walking to the lane, I knew that if I kept up a brisk step I could meet the last train to port. From there I could get the ferry to the mainland, and once there I'd make my way on the train again to London to meet Samuel, just as his letter said. This was an adventure — this was *mine* — and I was going to live it and love it, no matter what. But I was going now with the unexpected knowledge that my father was unknown to me and that my mother had . . . Never, not Ma. She was as prim as they come.

'Mairead!' The voice drifted on the air.

'Ma!' She stood there and looked at me whilst leaning over the fence and holding out a small package.

'Don't delay. You must go before your pa returns. He's for giving you a sound beatin' like none you ever had before. He took you in, my little Mairead, when others would have left you out for the wolves. Yet you turn your back on him, me . . . us.' She was not crying, but sniffed as the air had a cold edge to it, like her voice.

'Ma, is it true then? I'm a . . . ' I could barely think the word, let alone voice it to her, my own mother — for what did that make her?'

With her arms folded across the front of her pinny, she nodded. 'Aye, you are one in every sense of the word, it appears.'

My head and shoulders jolted back and I nearly lost my footing as she spoke. So that was why she hated me. She, the woman who had lain with another before being wed, blamed me for the sin. I was the result, and a constant reminder of her failings. Yet the pa who would now beat me in fury had kindly sheltered me as his own, and I never knew. I felt so sorry for him, not her or me, but for the man who had lived with a cuckoo in his nest for one and twenty years. He must truly love her.

'Who, then, is my father?'

She was shaking her head at me, her lips tightly shut in that defiant line I knew so well.

'I never knew that Pa was not my true father. Why didn't you tell me?'

'That's none of your business.'

'What? Of course it is. Why didn't he stay with you?' The last question fell from my lips before I thought of the implications or impact upon this woman who had been so distant to me my whole life, and yet now I knew a reason why. But to find out now, as I was leaving, and like this . . . it was cruel for both of us. I wanted to reach out and hug her, but then I had wanted to be able to do that for years without her brushing me away to do some chore.

'You've no idea. Your pa's a good man and he loves me. The man who sired you was not so. He was a brute and took what he wanted, and then I was left to raise his shame. If not for your pa, you would have been taken in by the sisters and I would have never held my head up again.'

'You were forced . . . ' I said. She swallowed and offered the small package again, ignoring my attempt at sympathy and understanding.

'Before I catch me death, take this and be gone. You are a stain that has tainted this family for long enough. The sisters should have taken you in and kept you as a nun. Then you would have had a goodly life and learnt to be grateful for the one you'd been given. Go to your Englishman and see if he is any better than the one who created you.'

I took the package and held her hand momentarily as I stared into her tired and bitter eyes.

'Ma, it wasn't my fault either, was it? I never asked to be born. Couldn't you have loved me and saved your hate for him?' I asked now for I might never get the chance again, but her mouth twisted into a half-smile as she shook her head.

'Love you, the evidence of my family's downfall?' She scoffed. 'You were there every day and he was never there again. The likes of us cannot touch the likes of him. I would've given you to the nuns, but Pa said that sometimes throwbacks happen, and that was how we'd explain that mass of dark hair. He's a good man and you have broken his heart. See, bad blood runs deep.'

I let her hand fall away from me. Her words cut me; time was slipping away, with the last touch of emotion that I could ever feel for this woman other than pity. But I knew I would write to

Pa — the only one who I had ever known and the only one who loved me so.

'Who was this man?' I asked one final time. He was rich and he was English, of this I was sure.

She took a step away from me, shaking her head and sneering. 'That you will never know. For he is nothing to you and would give you nothing in return if you pestered him. You've been raised poor and will stay that way. You have secured your fate.'

She ran back to the house.

I wasted no more time, and made for the station, keeping the small package carefully in my hand within the safety of my coat pocket. I would look at it when I had a calm moment again and space. Right now I wanted to go as far away as I could from the people who I had tended and loved, but now feared. Yet, my heart was splitting, for I ached to hug Pa and tell him I wish I'd known. But then there was a strange anxiety and curiosity taking hold of me.

Who was my real father? Did he even know I existed? Why would I seek him and ask him for anything? Why could he change me from being 'poor' — was he so rich?

With a head bursting with more questions than answers, I ran.

3

'Oh no! I've missed it.' I shouted the words out before I realised that I had done so. The tears that had been bubbling up inside me ever since Peggy and Ma's horrid revelations had cut me to the core and were now watering my eyes.

'No worries, lass.' I looked up at the smiling face of the man who appeared at my side. 'That was a post train, not a passenger one. That's due in ten minutes.' His reassurance helped my heart find its natural calm rhythm.

The stranger, a handsome young man, Ma would say, was finely dressed in a stylish hat and tweed jacket and matching trousers. He steadied me as I all but collapsed on the platform of the station, dropping the small bag at my feet.

'I thought . . . I'd . . . ' I took a deep

breath to compose myself, forced a smile onto my face and brushed away my doubt — or tried to. 'Not to worry.' I was going to walk down to the cheaper end of the platform.

'It's fine. Is it Dublin you're going to?' he asked, removing his hat and running his fingers through sandy curls. His hair looked just fine. It was not oiled down like Pa's; instead it bounced in short waves to his fringe with fashionably short sides.

I realised that he was still smiling at me. Like a fool, I was staring up at him into what I thought in this subdued light to be hazel eyes, a face framed by dusky blond hair with a dark brown fedora placed jauntily on top of his head. I swallowed and tried to sound confident. 'No . . . Liverpool.'

He laughed.

I felt awkward. What was so funny about Liverpool? Did he think I was lying?

'You'll be getting wet then, unless you know how to fly over the waters.'

I coloured. Of course I was to go to Dublin first. I was such a child, and he looked so confident and worldly. 'Yes, I obviously meant via Dublin.'

'Obviously.' He looked down the railway line. 'It will be here soon, miss.'

There were men gathering at the far end of the platform. They stumbled along and had been singing and laughing as they regrouped.

'Do you mind me asking what kind of ticket you have, miss?' He strolled over to where a leather suitcase had been left by a wooden seat a few steps away. In two strides he was back at my side, and I had to admit I was glad of his company. I had rarely ventured outside of our small village, and only once to the city with Pa when I was younger.

'Why do you wish to see my ticket?' I doubted him for no reason other than that this day was turning out to be one of my worst ever. In my mind, when planning this great adventure, it had been visualised in my mind as my liberation, my joy, my new life. Now it seemed I was all but destroyed. My father was not of my blood, and my mother thought I would become a wanton woman discarded on a dock-side. I had never felt so cold and alone.

'Well it is late now and you are on your own, and this is the last train, so you have no choice but to board it or spend a night here.' He had tilted his head as he looked at me. It was not a patronising gesture, but could I trust this man who I knew nothing about to have my genuine interest at his heart?

I showed him my ticket. He studied it, then glanced back at me and stared along at the bunch of men who were now singing merrily again. 'They've been at the Guinness, I think,' I said and smiled at him, but he continued to look down at me.

'Are you running away from home by any chance, miss?' he asked, and I stared back at him with indignation, suppressing the rising fear that was seeping into my veins.

'What business is that of yours? But no, I'm not. My ma waved me off with her blessing.' It was hardly a lie. I was in this so deep that I just had to see it through or I would be lost in a dark void; homeless, disowned and vulnerable.

The train steamed in and I was about to walk down to the lower end of the platform, boldly realising I would be the only woman surrounded by men who had had more than their share of liquid courage.

'Well, allow me.' He cupped my elbow, spun me around and walked to the carriage marked 'First'. He opened the door, and with whistles blowing, the train pulled away.

I was seated looking at him, clinging to my bag in front of me as though it was a defensive weapon or an impenetrable shield. But he just sat back, flipped his hat onto the empty long seat next to him and stared at me, still smiling.

'You'd get no peace in there, so enjoy

this time to rest and tell me why a pretty little thing like you is drifting around the Irish countryside making her way to Ireland's grandest port at night time unchaperoned.' He leaned back.

'I don't see what business it is of yours, sir,' I snapped my words back at him. 'Besides, it is evening, not night.' I sounded ill-tempered and he didn't deserve that, for all he had done was help me.

'Well it is, and the reason is simple — because I have made it so. You can protest, but I can tell a damsel in distress when I see one. Don't split hairs about the time; it is late and will be more so when you reach Dublin. Do you know that there are gangs that steal away passengers' bags at the dockside as they wait for the vessels, and then these 'runners' ask you to pay to get it back before you can board? People pay or go without.' He shrugged as if it was just the way of the world.

I stared, wide-eyed, at him; but then

as his words sank in, I had to brush a tear away from my right eye as it escaped my control. I had not thought about the hour I would arrive, just that I left in the daylight and then would wait for my passage in Liverpool. 'Who are these awful people who prey on the desperate who are about to embark on a new life in a foreign land? Why aren't they stopped?'

'They are also desperate or are just criminal in character. Either way, you would make easy pickings if you were to arrive — a lamb to the proverbial slaughter.'

'Are you trying to scare me?' I asked as I fought the panic that now threatened to consume me. 'There are more good people in this world than bad.' My words caused him to think solemnly for a moment.

'Miss, I lost an uncle in the Great War. I doubt the ratio of good to bad that you have such faith in.'

My eyes widened as I stared at him, not knowing how to respond.

'So what is your story, miss?' he asked, with arms folded.

It was then I saw the gold watch chain and the signet ring on his finger. He was certainly from a well-off background. So what was he doing bothering with me? I suspected he was maybe five summers older than me. He tilted his head again, amusement written over his features. Perhaps he was just bored and wanted someone to pass the journey with.

'It is nothing to you. I think you should content yourself with your own business.'

'For the moment, you are my business.' He laughed. 'Like I said, I have made you so.'

Something inside me ached to tell him. To share with him the fact I was not just a lost waif, but a young woman on a life's mission. I was going to be a wife and adventurer, and my world would be so broad that he could never dream of it.

'Well?'

'Very well. I am meeting my fiancé and we are emigrating to the Straits of Malaysia.' I spoke with confidence as the descriptions of the journey and the plantations came flooding back into my mind. Where miles and miles of rubber plantations replaced the older forestry that had stood like buttresses and reached up to the sky above the height of a cathedral, like God's church of nature. These had been pushed back to make way for the new order. Samuel had such a turn of phrase. There were birds with vibrant feathers and songs that cheered the angels, great monkeys so orange they called them orangutans or some such, and flowers that were brighter than the sun and redder than the reddest moon. Fruits so odd and some that smelled so strange only the locals would eat them. However, I longed to see it all for myself. When I closed my eyes on a night, I saw the colour, felt the humid heat, and heard the sounds of bullfrogs, crickets and the song of birds.

His eyebrows rose. 'That is not the reply I thought to hear.' His expression was troubled and serious for a moment.

'What did you think to hear?' I asked this nosey man.

'That you thought Liverpool's filthy streets shone with the brightest gold that reflected back to the sky the rays of the moon each night.' He waved his hands wide and then swooped them up towards the ceiling of the carriage as if it were the sky. With his hair being the colour of sunshine, the analogy suited him fine.

I laughed. 'You talk nonsense. You think I know nothing!'

'It is what I thought you would say, but I am impressed that you did not. You are a lady on a mission, yet you have no ring. Do you speak the truth?' Those eyes, so earnest, almost made me feel guilty even though I spoke God's honest truth.

'If this train stopped, I would get out now!' I said, and inched to the front of my seat as if I could get out.

'Sit back, lass. You are a sparky one. I have just saved you from a fate that would turn your cheeks cerise if I were to explain it to you, and yet you get tetchy with me.' He shook his head. 'Women folk!'

'You have the cheek to ask me so many questions, yet you have not said who you are and what you are doing here, 'rescuing damsels in distress' as you put it.'

'No, I haven't; but then you have not asked me, have you?'

He was enjoying himself so much that it looked as if the grin was going to fall off the sides of his wide jaw. He had straight teeth, no stain of baccy. Some lasses would fall for his looks and charms, but I had my Samuel and I would not be so easily turned.

'So who are you? Where are you going? Why?' I folded my arms in front of me, sat back and waited for him to divulge his information. I was more than curious, but had been too shy to ask, though not now. I had every right to, and it felt so strange and liberating. Would this be what my life would be like from now on? But then I remembered the letter in my pocket. Burnt and discarded. It would have the detail of where I was to go to meet my Samuel, and I had not even read it. I slipped my hand over it and was going to pull it out when I remembered it was obviously charred. I raised my eyebrows to this annoying stranger as if to say, 'Well?' waiting for him to answer; but he closed his eyes and simply said, 'Rest. We'll talk later.'

4

I watched his eyelids; they were so heavy with the need for sleep that it was predictable they would close. It seemed intrusive to stare at him, and yet I could not help myself. He had a kindly face, but I had not realised that those shadows under his eyes spoke of wakeful nights. Despite a well-defined chin and lips that readily smiled, I realised that his eyes revealed another emotion; they showed they had been sad of late.

His highly polished leather brogues had good soles. No hobnails in them to make them last. He could obviously afford to replace them when they wore out — if he kept them that long. The leather-bound suitcase matched them well in quality. He had tucked it alongside his feet. It had travelled well by the look of it; its worn look was at odds with the new shoes. The initials *E.J.R.*

could be just made out across one scuffed corner. Normally, if something is so used I would presume it was old and the owner poor, but this piece of luggage stood testament to being well-travelled, more so than its younger owner could be for sure. Still, I had more to think on than wasting time pondering on what his business could be.

Samuel's letter was in my hand and I was burning to read it. The last one promised details of where we would meet in England, and before that where I would collect my ticket for the crossing from Dublin to Liverpool. Once there, I was to find the offices of his agents and they would give me the details of our crossing and where I could meet him. We would marry by special licence and then within days board our ship to a whole new life. The overwhelming emotions that swept through me filled my heart as though it would burst. I was to start my new life as Mrs Blackman, and from that point there would be no more Maddie

Mulligan and her make-do life. It was as if I was to be washed clean of all that was sad and bad of my past. How many people had that chance?

I half-smiled at my shameful thoughts of sharing my life — myself — with my husband. I so wanted to be happy. Yet with such a heavy heart at my final parting from home, my benevolent 'pa' and my bitter ma, and then Peggy's unrivalled loathing of me, I could not lift my mood.

Taking out the precious piece of paper, I silently unfolded it and leaned to the window to read its words in the failing light.

His handwriting was immaculate, but his words were sometimes incorrect. This letter was to be no different; in fact the words were definitely wrong in their entirety. From the very first greeting, something about it made me uneasy.

My Dear Mairiud

I stifled the urge to laugh out loud; Ma would have forty fits if she knew he had not spelt my name correctly. I continued reading.

I have been thinking hard, and realised that I am the biggest of rogues, for I have filled your head, which I have no doubt is as beautiful as the soul who transposes her words so well, with dreams of far-off lands and bright colourful places, when I have no right to.

You have a loving home and family, and I am just a simple lonely man who has worked hard and now wishes to seize my chance at carving a career in my uncle's firm. Giles, Magdalene and Simms, Straits Rubber Plantation is offering me the chance to begin again. I have dreamt of this moment for three long years as I suffered the harsh realities of my indentures to an institution in the City of London. Now qualified, I can take up my post as an assistant on one of the Johor Bahru estates in Malaya. I must, therefore, depart early. This breaks my heart and will no doubt yours too.

I know in our essence we are as soulmates, but alas we can never make that final commitment to each other as we had planned, as I could never ask you to complete that perilous journey on your own. It would be a sin in so many ways.

So it is with an aching heart and a guilt-ridden spirit, my dear M, that I must write these words. Fate has decreed we are not to meet. You see, what could have been simply was not to be. You are so obviously gifted with your words, and creative of mind, that you will make some deserving man a fine wife. That man is not me.

I must, therefore, send you my absolute and sincerest good wishes in order to guarantee that this final letter reaches you before you make that bold and perhaps ill-considered parting and set off on what is now a shattered dream.

Your humble and apologetic friend,
S. Blackman Esq.

I stared at the paper and could not believe what I had just read. This could not be. It left me with nowhere to go. To stay in Dublin was no choice. To continue without the ticket that was promised would be beyond my means, and to return would be unbearable.

No, there was something false about this letter; more than the false promises that he had made. It was not true to his voice — it was wrong in tone. Something of it sounded distant and insincere. There was no talk of the poetry of the journey ahead. Where was all the enthusiasm for what he was to experience?

Was I to accept that he had been leading me on some sort of wild goose chase? That I had been nothing more to him than an amusement to fill in his 'lonely' days whilst he worked hard and achieved his own ends? No, I could not believe that this turn of events was true. I knew my heart did not want it to be so, but my Samuel was not that kind of man. There was too much detail in his previous letters for him to simply dismiss me in this way.

The tone of this was patronising, as if I were no more than a foolish whimsical child and he the spinner of sweet fairytales. We were more than this. Someone had the detail in the original, perhaps, to make me believe this substituted letter in the hope I should return home contrite, forever to atone and serve.

Then a thought struck me — what if Samuel was not well?

The tears that ran silently down my cheeks as the train jolted landed on my wrist as I held the paper, and I lurched forward before sinking back into the seat. I was so tired. Emotions had run through my system like water down a drain, and I had been left devoid of all.

If Samuel had not realised that I had not received his last letter with his instructions, how was I to know where to collect my ticket to Liverpool? If I could make it that far, I could go to the agents and find out the truth of where he was and if I could still meet him.

My hand was trembling so much that I could hardly read the horrid words in front of me. It was only when it slid through my fingers and I wiped my blurred vision that I realised that the stranger opposite was reading my private letter. Wiping my eyes with the hanky I had ironed only hours earlier for my voyage, I tried to compose myself and look at him with some remnants of dignity — but I felt naked and exposed and my emotions were raw.

'That's my personal property; you've no right to . . . ' My words petered out, as did my last resolve to protest to anyone about anything anymore.

'Yes, I do, Mairirud,' he said, deliberately mispronouncing my name. Even now there was humour in his words.

'You mock me when you can see that someone is trying to make a fool of me! What kind of man are you?' I asked, and swallowed. I had no bitterness or anger in my voice, just the absolute feeling of despair. My destiny was now such that I was about to arrive in a port city at night with no one to meet me, limited funds, and nowhere to go to get my onward ticket. I could not return home, not without a barrage of shame being heaped upon me that I could never recover from. How could I ever, after what I had done? Besides, now the realisation hit me that I had a night to spend in Dublin before a train would return to my small village. If I spent any money on my digs, then I could not go either forward or back when the next day dawned, as I had no idea how long it would be before I found work or digs in Dublin to pay my way — either way. I closed my eyes tightly shut for a moment to stop the tears from falling again and instead breathed in deeply. My body ached with all the worry and my head felt strange.

'Well, I am a better one than this one, for sure,' he said. 'You, miss, have been made destitute!'

My question had been rhetorical, and so when I heard him folding the letter back up, I reluctantly reopened my eyes and looked at him. How could I have fallen from being poor to destitute so quickly, and by my own doing? *Oh, Maddy, what a fool you are!* I remonstrated.

'How did you ever get into such a pickle with a man who would write in such a fashion? Where do you write to this man?' he asked.

It took a moment for me to realise he was asking for Samuel's address. 'Well, he has moved around. At first it was a London address, and then when he took his exams he returned to Dublin for a few months. The address on the back of that one just states Foley Street.' I saw the change of expression in the man opposite, and it made me wary. Why would he react so badly to the mention of a street?

'Good heavens!' His words were snapped out so sharply I was surprised. 'How he has fallen from grace.'

'You know it?' I asked. 'Why has Samuel fallen? He worked hard in London and qualified.'

'No, I do not know it personally — the address, that is — but I, like many, know *of* it. Miss, you have been duped and sorely used. For this man lives in a hovel, and that is no overstatement. The tenements are not a place I would inhabit by choice. In fact, I would not go anywhere near them.'

'Perhaps he had no choice,' I offered defensively, but then added, 'That letter was not written by him, I am certain.' He raised quizzical eyebrows at me, but my lips were set in a determined line. I knew Samuel's hand.

'I can see you have had a shock and that you do not want to believe the truth of this letter. But, miss, you must heed my words seriously. The animal gangs own those streets. They're . . . ' He shook his head. 'Do not ever think of tracing this address, Mairead.'

'Animal gangs?' I interrupted, ignoring his warning. 'What animals roam in Dublin?'

'Oh, lass!' He sighed. Leaning forward, he placed the letter on the seat next to me and took my hands in each of his. 'Human kind of animals — the worst!'

I let him hold my fingers. My world, my head was spinning.

'The IRA and the local lads fight for the rights to earn what little they can from selling papers and things.' He squeezed my fingers gently and I remembered to breathe. I refocused on his face, those handsome hazel eyes. 'They are brutal. You'll have heard of knuckle dusters, caps edged with razors, crow bars . . . ' His words trailed off as I stared at him blankly.

I shook my head silently.

'You cannot search this man out. No man in their right mind would enter as a stranger, let alone a slip of a lass, a pretty young woman like you.' He was gently massaging the back of my hands with his thumbs.

My head felt even stranger; his eyes were closing . . . No, it wasn't his eyes that were closing; it was . . .

'Come on, Mairead, sit up.'

I felt strong arms around me as I slumped forward. One minute there were words of advice drifting in my ears and the next they were floating, detached, above me. I realised as a world full of motion came back into my vision that I had blacked out. 'I'm sorry,' I muttered.

'Don't be, Mairead. You have had a shock. My explanation was perhaps too graphic.' He was standing — well, half-kneeling — over me, one hand resting on my shoulder to prevent me from listing forward against the train's motion.

'I am a fool,' I said. 'I shall throw myself on the mercy of the nuns. Samuel's letter, it burned in the hearth; this one has been substituted by my sister. It smacks of her bitterness and revenge. She would have me return to be forever a shamed servant to her and Ma. Damn them! Without Samuel's instructions on where to collect my ticket, I am lost.'

My eyes shot open when I heard his

laughter. He sat back on the edge of his seat.

'I'm sorry, but please do not throw yourself on the mercy of the nuns. I would not wish it upon an ugly wench, let alone one so fair as you. I have more knowledge on the subject than you may have, sweet Mairead.'

'My hair is anything but fair, as well you can see,' I rallied as I straightened my back again. My wits were returning with a burning sensation that was making my vision very clear indeed. I felt anger turning to silent rage that 'Samuel' could have duped me and played me for a fool. I would find him and show him how 'animal' my behaviour could be when riled! Then I looked at the paper again. No, I would find him and discover the truth of this. Something or someone had intervened. Those words were forced. They were not from his heart, of that I was certain. It has to be Peggy.

'It was not your hair I was referring to,' he replied. There was no broad smile this time; his look was pensive.

'What have you to do with nuns?' I asked.

'My uncle is a priest and my aunt a nun. I . . . ' He rubbed his face, and I could see his tired drawn expression. 'Oh, I may as well reveal my own dirty washing, as yours has been cast before me. I am a black sheep, a stain on a family that would disown me. I failed to carry out my father's wishes and become a priest. I have let the family down and heaped shame on my mother, or so she would have me believe. My two brothers are free to carry on the family name; and I, as a spare, was sent to train as a priest.' He shrugged. 'I simply could not do it. I made my money in business and returned after five long years — the prodigal to impress them — only to be told I died five years ago. They would not acknowledge me. So I return whence I came. I too am making my way to Liverpool.'

'Oh!' I said. His dilemma seemed as

dire as mine, except that he could obviously afford to do as he wished.

'Is that all you can say? See, I am no good at giving or taking confessions.' He laughed tiredly. This time the mirth was missing.

'You are being true to yourself,' I offered.

'Indeed; and it would appear that our paths were meant to cross. Perhaps we should work this mystery out together, as I have very little else to occupy me at this moment in time.'

It would not be easy to convince this Good Samaritan that come what may, Maddie Mulligan could take care of herself. Whether it was the anger or the newfound freedom that drove my determination, I was going to survive and triumph. I would meet this Samuel unless he had departed, and I would track him down in Liverpool using the offices of his uncle's firm. He might or might not be in reduced digs in Dublin, but that firm he had mentioned by name before. He had had a London address and he was real. I was now on a mission: to bring justice for Maddie Mulligan and the downfall of Samuel Blackman, if he had indeed played me false.

'Thank you, but I think you have enough to contend with without adding my problems to yours.'

'No, miss . . . What is your true name?' he asked.

'Miss Mairead Mulligan,' I revealed and then asked, 'And yours?'

'Mr Connor Riley. My uncle is the priest in your village, I believe. He, too, blanked my existence.'

'Well, Mr Riley . . . '

'Connor,' he said, and shrugged. 'We can dispense with formalities as we are both outcasts.'

'Very well, Connor. If I accept your charity this night — I mean to keep me safe; I am not offering . . . ' I did not know what I was saying; but as the train approached the station, I was filled with a fear like nothing I had known before, and I needed his help.

'We shall be safe this night, you and I, and I will not take advantage of you or your situation; and likewise I would ask you do not do that with me.' He winked at me and I laughed.

5

Connor jumped up from his seat as soon as the train pulled in. I was nervous, but he pushed down the window and turned the handle of the door releasing it from outside. The cold air swept in as it flew open.

'Your future has just begun, Miss Mairead Mulligan!' he declared, and then took my hand in his and helped me to climb down onto the platform.

The Great Southern Railway train pulled into the once great Broadstone Station. I had heard in the shop from the delivery man who brought newspapers to the village that this grand building was going to be abandoned, as the old canals were no longer needed that somehow linked to it. It was all gossip overheard from visitors to the village shop when supplies were delivered. That was how important news travelled from village to village, by word of mouth — a snippet here, a snippet there. The knowledge made no sense to us most of the time and was distorted in the retelling, but at least I knew something of the place where I had arrived.

I did not argue with Connor as to which way to go, or where I should stand. This was like a new land to me, with high stone buildings and broad roads. It was busy even at this hour. I clung to my bag. 'Do we walk from here?' I asked.

He smiled at me and shook his head. Instead of answering, he took me straight to an automobile that was parked alongside the road. Confidently, he paid the driver and told me to climb inside. I did and it smelt of polished leather.

I was feeling excited, tired and anxious all at the same time. My dream had been shattered. My journey to meet my lover, instead of being a precarious one on a ferry to his welcoming arms, had become a very different kind of adventure — one that had polished leather seats, where I was being driven around a city as if I were a lady. The notion made me smile self-consciously, as I had never thought myself to be so grand. We travelled down streets; some neared an area where they narrowed and the dim night seemed even darker ahead. They looked rough. Those buildings were high but seemed crammed. I wondered if that was where Foley Street was, but then we turned away and headed down broader avenues until we stopped outside what I could only describe as a grand house. The windows were as tall as doors and the roof higher than any tree I had ever seen before. In the compound at the front were four trees. Each would have looked grand by the village green, yet here they were surrounding a well kept garden in a private enclosure.

'Come on in, Mairead,' he said, and offered me a hand as we left the vehicle and he opened the iron gate to this private land. 'The night's cold, and in that thin coat you'll catch a chill.'

I stifled a laugh, as he could have been my ma, only his words were caring and not sharp and critical. The 'thin coat' was the warmest garment I possessed. It had started out as Ma's many years before.

The clang of the automobile door closing behind us made me jump, but Connor just took my hand again; and with my other hand desperately clinging to the last vestige of my old life, we ran up to the door.

He released me, only to fidget around in his pocket before retrieving and turning the key in the lock and throwing the large black door wide open. 'Go on in; the night's cold and I'm nearly ready for my bed.'

I did not hesitate and stepped inside. However, his words lingered in my mind. What was he talking to me about bed for?

The hallway appeared to be mostly carved out of wood. Every aspect of it had once grown in a forest. The floor was made up of patterns of tiles. Strips of different types of wood that had been polished and placed in slanted patterns made up the beautiful flooring. The walls were lined in oak panels or some such, and ahead the carpeted stairs were also made of the same. I stared around me in wonder. I'd never seen such a place. The grandest building I'd been in before this was the church, and that was made mainly of stone. That had been cold and austere, yet this house felt homely.

Closing the door firmly behind me, he placed his suitcase down by a tall hall stand and walked towards the back of the house, where there was a door that led to a short corridor and down to a kitchen.

'Mrs O'Malley doesn't come in on a weekend, so we'll have to make ourselves a drink and find something to eat.' He took off his hat and coat and draped them over a painted kitchen chair.

'Mrs O'Malley,' I repeated as he

filled a kettle and placed it on the stove. It was a special stove where flames happened at a click of a button and the touch of a flame. It felt like I had come from a hovel into the civilised world; except for what he had told me about Foley Street and the tenements, this world was not in the grasp of everyone. This was no tenement — this was a rich man's house, and I had agreed to stay in it. The realisation hit me and I turned to leave. It felt like I had sold my soul — not once, but twice over, this night.

'Don't leave, Mairead. You really would be a lost soul out there, and easy for the picking. No one is in this house who is here to judge you. No eyes to spy on either of us — believe me, I know all about that. I am my own man.' He looked casually over at me as he took two cups and plates out of a cupboard. They were china ones and matched. 'You can relax here, for you are safe with me.'

All the while he spoke, he continued

to make me tea, cut a slice of bread from a fresh loaf and spread it with butter and honey. 'Here, it's not much, but it'll tide you over till morning.'

'Are you really so bored that you want to bother with me? I don't belong here, Connor. I was born into a poor worker's home.' I looked at the lace-edged doilies that were stacked neatly on a shelf, the silver tea service in a glass cupboard, and the copper pans hanging on hooks from the ceiling over the stove.

'Why should I be bored to think to bother with you? Because you have been brought up to believe you should stay put where you were born? Be honest, Mairead . . . '

'Maddie,' I corrected.

'Maddie, you have broken free of that bond and doctrine. So your freedom has not happened as you expected it to — yet we are now on an adventure, you and I, are we not? Never let anyone tell you that you belong to the circumstances you were born to. The rich think it's their right, and the poor believe foolishly it's their lot in life. Well I say you make of life what you can, if you dare. Do you dare to change yours?'

I nodded.

'Good, because you already have!'

I laughed, and he looked surprised. 'Your words may not be what a priest might say, but you deliver your message with equal passion and conviction,' I said, and saw his cheeks quickly flush. He looked away thoughtfully for a moment before replying to me.

'I am not offended, but passion does not mean I wish to drive a doctrine down people's throats. I have been practically excommunicated from the family that raised me, and you have left yours behind. So we stay here, eat, and look at the facts as you know them about this man that seems to have cut you off — or we shall also look at the possibility that the letter was destroyed, and this is a poor replacement created to drive you back to your old life of serving your family in shame and humility. I shall fetch a pencil and paper and we will write down everything you know about this man, and together let us see if we can trace your Mr Samuel Blackman. The truth is ours to find. It is quite an intriguing prospect.' He disappeared from the room as I began to eat and drink.

Connor returned, as good as his word, with the implements to take down the detail of my folly in a notebook before him.

'I shall eat first,' he declared. 'You begin at the beginning. With my help, we shall unearth God's honest truth of it.'

I shook my head as he beamed his all-encompassing smile at me. He had an easy appealing manner to him. I would be surprised if he lived in this big house on his own. Yet, if he had a wife he would hardly be wasting his time with me. Perhaps he was another lost soul, as he painted himself.

'You are tired and sad, Connor.' The

words poured from my lips without hindrance. Maybe because I was tired, I did not think to censor them.

'That is why I want to help you, Maddie. You are honest. You do not judge me. I told you I walked away from the church and a 'calling', and you said not one word against me. I do not wish to judge you either. I am sad because my family would rather drive me out than listen to why I would be miserable if I did as they wished and followed the life of a priest.' He bit his bottom lip as if to stop it from trembling.

'But it was not your 'calling', was it? So you are following what you are meant to do. God or your heart is leading you down a different path, Connor. Perhaps you were meant to help me and save me from a life of abject poverty and sin,' I said, and then felt my cheeks burn as I acknowledged what a huge part he had played in my future.

He laughed, and I told him everything I could remember about the letters. I had not kept them, for Peggy or Ma would have found them. There were no secrets hidden in our small home. So I read each three times, committed the words to my memory, and burnt each in turn. We must have exchanged as many as eight letters in the year.

He took notes as I recalled any details, and then yawned before putting the pencil down.

'Maddie, it is time we slept. We'll wash these pots in the morning and discuss these notes then. A fresh and rested brain can think so much more quickly than a tired one.' He stood and led the way back up to the oak staircase and began climbing the stairs. I stood at the bottom with bag in hand. I suddenly did not know what to do or say.

He never even looked back down at me. 'You can sleep in the hall if you wish, or you can use my pious sister's room. Since she is now a nun, she no longer needs her things, so feel free to pull out a nightdress and gown from the wardrobe. The door is second on the right at the top of the stairs. The bathroom adjoins and the doors lock from the inside. Good night, Maddie. Breakfast will be at 8 a.m. I'll shout at 7:30 a.m. Sleep well.'

He continued walking, and I slowly climbed the stairs after him.

6

The room was beautiful. What struck me first about it was that it was light despite having two heavy pieces of furniture against the wall. I think they might have been made of walnut wood, dark but warm and patterned in the grain, but it was only a guess. It had a four-poster bed in the middle of the wall opposite the tall window. I thought of the bed that I had shared with my two sisters at home and shook my head. We could have fitted the boys on this one as well. If Ma and Pa had had one like this then, I chuckled, there would have been more siblings, no doubt. Yet all this space was for one woman.

I walked slowly in, as if I would be accused of trespassing. It was the detail of the fabrics that caught my attention. They were cream with embroidered birds all over them. Flowers and leaves were woven into the design so that they made their way down the fabric. The same pattern was all over the curtains, and the paper on the wall was covered in a delicate cherry-blossom pattern. It had an exotic feel to it. The birds and the flowers were not like any I had seen in Ireland. They were colourful, delicate and oh so pretty. The blossom and fruit looked as though I would be able to taste them or smell their sweet perfume.

The tall cupboard and chest of drawers that lined the wall provided a solid wood contrast to the delicate stitching of the drapes and bedcovers. I stood and shook my head in disbelief. Why would anyone ever turn their back on such luxury to live the lonely and strict life at a convent? I had no notion, and that just made me realise how lacking I was. It was obvious that I had no calling in me at all. Was this the sinful work of the devil, as Ma would say? These things were thoughts higher than mine. I just felt that whatever we were blessed with, we should gratefully enjoy; and I intended to do that here, if only for one night in my life.

The bed felt soft. A feather mattress, I suspected. I smiled through tired eyes that blurred with emotion as I flopped on top of it and tossed my worn-out shoes onto the floor. My tired feet felt so relieved to be free of them. They almost felt warmer out of them than they had inside.

My hat lay next to me on the bed, and my bag had been discarded on a chair by the door. I meant to go into the small room attached to this one and wash, but I was overcome by an irresistible urge. I closed my eyes and drifted. I imagined that this was all mine and that I could eat here, dress here, live here and go out and help the poor by providing soup and fine bread as a thank-you for the blessing of this life. I drifted so far, so deep and long that the first I knew of morning was when a voice very close to me resonated in my ear, repeating my name. It was the feel of a strange hand gently rocking my shoulder that brought me back to consciousness though.

'Maddie!'

I sat up too quickly, instantly felt dizzy, and nearly fell off the side of the high bed. Strong arms encircled me and lifted me back on top.

Connor's face was close to mine as he sat me on the bed, propped up against him. I breathed deeply and recovered. His hand cupped my chin and I gasped.

'I thought you were unconscious. My goodness, you poor thing. You must have been here like this all night. You must be freezing. I should not have left you like I did.' He leaned me back against the pillow.

'I'm so sorry . . . ' I began to explain, but he put up the palm of his hand to tell me to be silent.

Next he bent down out of sight, and I heard a click and the noise of escaping air or gas. I looked up and saw that he had lit a fire of sorts in the grate. It flickered and spluttered slightly, but the warmth it gave out was instant. He then started to pull open drawers and the wardrobe. No peat fires here, I mused.

I looked on in awe as he pulled out new undergarments, stockings, shift, underskirt and a tweed suit in a beautiful blue weave. From a top shelf he took down a navy beret and pair of gloves to match.

'They may be a little roomy on you,' he said in a slightly apologetic in tone as he looked over at me, 'for you are thin, Maddie. But I am sure that will only make the outfit look even more stunning.' He smiled. 'They are all lined, so will be warmer than that rough-weave suit you were wearing. You go wash and change. The water closet is just next to the bathroom, so see to your needs first and I'll be down in the kitchen. I'll bring your breakfast tray up here, and we can discuss our first plan of attack. Oh . . . ' He pulled out a small leather suitcase and tossed it on the bed. 'I suggest you repack into that one, as yours looks like the handle is about to go on a journey on its own.'

He winked at me, so I did not take offence. 'Find another change of underthings and select another one of her suits. I don't know if the shoes will fit, but if they do then help yourself. They will just collect dust if you don't. We may well need to cross to Liverpool to find your man. So best go as quickly as you can, as you don't want to miss the ferry.'

I watched as he opened the door. 'Connor, I can't take these things. I can never repay you; and besides, they are not yours to give.' I felt awful saying this, but it sounded as though he was giving away his sister's things behind her back, and I could not be a party to that. No matter how beautiful and tempting they were.

'Yes, you can and you will! You see, Maddie, yes they are mine, for she never accepted my gifts. They have never been worn — any of them. She obeyed her parents and instead of choosing my worldly path, she chose to ignore the gift of speech that her Father up in Heaven had given her and all the lovely things I had worked so hard to buy for her, and now I am left with this.' He shook his head and waved his hands around the room. The hurt was written on his face. 'I nearly threw it all at the door of the tenements for the poor to fight over, but if I had they may well have caused bloody disputes. So I left all where I had put them for her to find.'

His words were harsher and snapped out in a way that he had not used with me before.

'Maddie, I do not want to live with a shrine to someone who has rejected me also. I would rather see someone who is deserved of it enjoy these things. That is not unfair, is it? Can I not experience the joy of giving and feel the reward of your joy at accepting them?' He laughed at my bemused face. 'It is your Christian duty to receive, so that I may give!'

'Why me?' I asked. I shook my head.

'Because my faith — and I do have

one — tells me that you are the reason why I was turned away from home and why I caught that same train as your good self. You, dear Maddie, are the soul I am to save. So like it or not, you have my undivided attention until we find this Samuel and I can wish you both a happy and healthy life in a far-off land.'

'What if we don't find him?' I asked, wondering how much better life could be in the 'far-off land' than this home right here. There were so many people in need that surely ... I stopped my train of thought because it sounded like something calling me. It had everything anyone could wish for — except love, perhaps; but Connor seemed to have more than his share of that. He was the kindest person I ever had met.

He placed a hand over his lips as if shocked that the thought had never occurred to him that we might never find Samuel. 'Then, my dear Maddie, we will have a new dilemma to solve.' He looked at me and opened the door.

'We will cross that proverbial bridge once it has come into our vision; until then we stick to the first plan. Find your man; and if he turns out to be a cad, my dear Maddie, I will mete out some justice on your behalf. Now, hurry — we have a ferry to catch.'

'I would never forgive myself if you got hurt in a fight, Connor.' I raised my voice as anxiety swept through me. He had vanished from my sight, but must have heard my cry, for he popped his head back around the doorway.

'My dear Maddie, if someone who has sat at a desk for years can beat Connor Riley in a fight, then I would not have deserved all of this. Hurry now,' he said, and left.

His words lingered in my head until I opened the small door next to the bathroom and saw the water closet. Such luxury! The wooden seat was polished well, so that it felt warm. No need to break the ice in the outhouse here! The taps in the bathroom ran warm water too. A block of soap smelt like lavender, and I could not resist it. Using the soft square of towelling that was at the side, I stripped naked and washed everywhere. I even washed my hair and wrapped it in the crisp thin towelling sheet. I felt warm and clean, like I'd not for so long. I washed the remnants of my dirty water away and dressed by the fire. The silk undergarments felt so sinful, but made me well up with joy. The blouse was cream and had pearl-like buttons on it. The skirt swivelled loosely around my hips, but it would do. I rolled the stockings up. I'd even used the razor in the bathroom to make my legs as naked as they could be, and I was glad that I did because the stocking glided over my smooth skin.

I hung my head upside down and rubbed my hair as dry as I could with the towel by the heat of the fire. I had not realised that Connor had returned until I swooped my hair over my head as I stood upright again. He seemed frozen in the moment, tray in hands, and I stood likewise with the towel in mine. Our eyes met and for a moment we did not speak.

He coughed. 'Aye, good, lass. You brush that beautiful mane of yours out, and I'll pour the coffee. Do you like it with milk or black?' He coughed and put the tray down on the table. I smiled as I did as he asked and then fixed my almost dry hair up into a bun.

'Milk, please, I think. We always have tea.'

'Do you not like coffee?' he asked.

'I will love it, but I have never tasted it before.'

He poured some milk into the coffee and brought the cup over to me. 'Welcome to the new world, Miss Mairead Mulligan. The future has just begun.'

I took the cup from his hand and sipped the liquid. It was fresh, warm, different and I loved it as I stared into Connor's eyes and realised we had better find Samuel fast, because I was beginning to like more than the coffee far too much.

7

'So you stay here and I will go to the ticket office and see if any word has been left for you there.' He looked pensive for a second. 'Maddie, it is possible we will not find a message, or any trace of the man or any sign of him existing. I cannot promise that this will have a happy ending — but we will find the truth, or as near to it as we possibly can.'

'He exists! I have written to him these past twelve months, Connor. You must believe me, for you have seen the letter yourself.'

'I do not doubt that, but he could be a figment of someone else's mind. He may not be real, this Samuel Blackman. It could all be some kind of game to play with an innocent's heart.' He raised his eyebrows and I shook my head.

'I know it all seems strange and convoluted, but he exists, I feel it. You are being a true gentleman. That is more than I can ask or expect. Thank you, for I know without your help I would be lost, and — '

'And nothing. You've given me something to 'bother' about, haven't you? As for 'true gentlemen', stay clear of them. In my brief experience, they are less than they are being cracked out to be.'

'Why do I need to stay here? I want to come too,' I said as I swept up the last crumb of the toast that accompanied my eggs. I loved them; they had some sauce that tasted vaguely of mustard over them, poached in a way that the yolk stayed runny yet the white was set firm. 'Have you trained as a cook?' I asked, distracted by the sensation of tastes that had filled my mouth from such a simple plate of food.

He laughed and I saw his eyes fill with joy. 'You are priceless, Maddie!' he replied. 'No, I just like good food, and whenever I stay in a place that provides a dish I love, I make sure to learn how to make it. I have been blessed never to have been hungry, like I suspect you have, and I rejoice in my good fortune. My mother, although she lives like a fine lady now in her own house, was a child of such a place as the tenements. She lived seven in a small room and lost three sisters to pleurisy and pneumonia before they reached four. I promised she would never know that life again. Ironically, she put this down to God's will and not my hard work and effort. So, although I accept it may be both, I cannot but feel aggrieved that she has not been more grateful to me. Instead, the result is I enjoy my life and my food, and am too selfish to give it over to live a sham and empty life pretending to be a devout priest.' He shrugged. 'Now she has chosen to lose a son. Some people will never take or accept the easy route through life when presented with it. I, to put it bluntly, am not cut out to have a celibate life.'

I could not help but laugh, for with his warm nature and attractive looks I could not help but think it would be the waste of a good man. God forgive me for thinking like Eve, but if it were not for my agreement with Samuel, I could do much worse than considering the man opposite me right now. I could feel my cheeks colouring, so changed my train of thought quickly. 'You learn well.' I pointed to my now empty plate. 'Our past is steeped in famine and sorrow, you know it, and so I will take a different path if it is presented, as long as my soul does not have to be sold along the way.'

'Ah, hold on to that my girl, for without it you'd be truly lost!'

He waved a warning finger at me as if he were an admonishing priest, and I smiled. His spirit was light and infectious. How different to those of folk at home.

'Were you always rich, then, or has this all come by your own hand? You said that you had provided this for your sister, but how? You never told me what 'business' you were in.' I felt I should know the truth of it if I were to accept his offerings so willingly — and I was so willing after feeling quality cloth against my skin.

'No, that's true, I didn't,' he replied quickly. 'We don't have time for all of that right now; we only have time to sort your problems out. I'll tell you of my errant ways one day, but not today.' He winked impishly and I shook my head. One minute he seemed full of mischief and was young and playful; the next he had that air of sadness about him that he was obviously trying to fight off. Yet he had the confidence and voice of authority of a person years older than he was. How many of life's hardships had those lovely eyes seen that he masked behind a warm smile? I wondered. Charm, though, he had in abundance.

I did not know where my new courage was coming from, but I spoke my mind. This was my life he was sorting out, so I thought I had a right to be there too. 'I want to go with you.' I repeated my request firmly. 'I do not wish to be left out of my own 'adventure'.'

'The docks are no place for a beauty such as you to hang around. Not unless you were . . . ' He cleared his throat and then continued. 'I will go, buy the tickets if indeed they need to be bought, and you shall await my return. Because time slips away so quickly, I suggest that we make our way there. I will leave you with the driver and we shall continue our adventure. You have packed, I see,' he said as he noted the suitcase placed by the door. 'Save your questions for now. You already have too many to find answers for of your own.'

'Very well. I will wait until some of my own are answered, and then I will pursue more of yours.' I looked down at my feet, hardly believing that the shoes upon them were mine to enjoy. 'Yes, the shoes are a little roomy, but that is much better than nipping like my old damp ones did. They haven't been re-soled twice either,' I added.

'You remind me of a time long ago in my own life, when I knew someone who had very little. I was not in a position to help her then, but I can you. So here ... ' He walked over to a cupboard that was built into the wall. This house could contain families, yet he seemed to live in it on his own with the visitation of a woman to do for him. 'Here, add these to your lot and do not thank me, just enjoy them.' He opened the cupboard door and brought out a pair of laced-up ankle boots in the finest tan leather I had ever seen. Without stopping for me to say anything, he opened the suitcase and laid them on the top. 'I had them made especially,' he said, and actually swallowed back some powerful wave of emotion. 'They have never been worn and are the same size as the ones on your feet.'

'Connor . . . ' I was about to ask him if he was sure about this gesture of generosity, but he turned around and cut me off.

'Finish what you are to do. I will be

downstairs waiting for you.' He picked up the case in one hand and the tray in the other. 'You bring yourself, coat, hat and gloves downstairs and we shall go.'

I nodded and quickly brushed out my hair before fixing it properly and placing the beret atop it. The coat slipped over the suit, its lining so smooth it almost glided into place. The gloves added the final touch. I turned to walk to the door, but caught my reflection in the long mirror. I stopped, frozen at first in shock, because I honestly believed that this was a stranger staring back at me. As if his sister had materialised and was about to scorn me for daring to steal her things — yet it was me. I looked so . . . so . . . pretty . . . elegant, even. The realisation made me feel quite numb. I had become someone I did not even recognise; but I liked so much about what I saw that it pleased me beyond delight. If this was my future, I would never look back.

'Maddie!' The shout brought my wits back to me.

'Yes . . . coming!' I yelled, and ran down the stairs to see Connor staring at me as I approached him. I could see appreciation in his eyes, and some of the same awe that I had witnessed in my own expression. I stood straight and held my head up high.

'Come on then,' I said cheekily, and marched past him out into the Dublin air. I heard him stifle a chuckle.

'Yes, Miss Mulligan,' he said, and locked the door before overtaking me to open the large iron gate. The automobile was waiting with its engine chugging away. The driver opened the door and lowered a step for me to climb in. I noticed that he had a scar on his cheek that looked as though it had been from a nasty gash at some point. Our eyes never met as he saw to his duty. He only looked Connor straight in the eye when they spoke.

This was grander than anything I could have ever imagined. How could Samuel ever better this? I stepped forward into my future, wanting desperately to leave my past behind, but already struggling to come to terms with how much I loved this present state of being. With Connor seated beside me, we clashed as the car turned a sharp corner, and linked arms, grinning like children at each other. We were both blanking our family troubles and finding a reason to be busy and happy. If I could have stopped time in this moment, I think I would have, because for the first time in years I felt cared for and happy. His sandy fringe fell over one eye and I flicked it away with one finger. He took hold of my fingers and gently gave them a kiss. Our eyes met and we stared at each other, no words were spoken; but my heart felt alive in a way I had not known before.

'To the ferry offices as quick as the wheels will take us,' Connor ordered, and the car moved off at speed.

I felt awkward as he released my hand and so stared out of the window. It was not the gesture that had made me feel that way, but the separation. It felt right when we touched. It felt right when we stared honestly at each other; it felt right being in this man's strange world, his sister's clothes. And yet, we were as strangers. Then I realised that I had promised so much more to a man I had never met before. What if I did not feel the same when he touched me? I swallowed. I felt as though I had been as a child living a dream, following a path that had been written down for me to believe, like a storybook. Yet, the realisation that was before me now in this beautiful of contrasts could have dealt me a far more dangerous situation.

I glanced at Connor, who was staring out of the opposite window. He, too looked locked in his own thoughts. How soon would this lost soul stand me before he became bored with his new adventure?

No, I would not think like a child again. His story was already written for him. He was a man who has made his wealth, by what means I knew not, but he was being magnanimous and humble at the moment because he was suffering rejection. Once his personal grief at the loss of a family drifted off, and anger and determination to carry on with his life returned, I had no doubt that Maddie would be a distant memory. So I held my new gloves on my lap and was grateful that the timing of our meeting was beneficial for both of us. It was no more than that, a meeting of circumstance.

The scenery changed, and I could see high cranes lifting huge bundles of goods onto the ships that were docked. The noise of machinery, men shouting, chains clanging and hammers pounding resonated as we entered the dockside. People milled around. Steam billowed, and penned cattle and sheep could be heard in the distance as they were systematically channelled down high-sided gangplanks to the cattle boat. All the smells and noises of humanity filled the crisp damp air. I had opened the window of the automobile as it stopped. Connor slipped it shut again. A boat seemed to be grabbing the bottom of the harbour and dredging it in the distance as it made its way along the channel.

'Stay here, Maddie. I shall return very shortly. This catch locks the door from the inside. You keep them locked. If anyone is a bother, the driver will sort it. You sit back and just stay out of sight, yes?' he said.

'Very well,' I agreed. I was looking past his head, but was watching a large load that was being swung high in the air in the distance. I did not mean to ignore him, but was very distracted. Connor did not seem to notice.

He left us, and I saw men walking and waiting at the side. They must be waiting for work, I thought. They had a drawn look of defeat upon them. Their flat caps could not hide the expression of dejection as the younger fitter workers had obviously been chosen for the day. After some moments, a grubby face appeared at the window, tapping on the glass and holding a hand out. I could read his words from his lips. He wanted money, but I had none to give. The pennies I had for my original voyage were all in my case in the boot of this vehicle, and they were not so many that I could afford to give them away. Yet, sitting here I looked like the lady that I was not, in an automobile that I did not own and dressed in new clothes. I shook my head, but the man's anger became worse. He slammed the palm of his hand against the window. That was enough for the driver to react. He stood outside the vehicle with an iron bar in his hand and raised it at the unfortunate man, exchanging words that I don't think ever appeared in the Bible. At first the man protested and did not move away; but when the driver, a large man, raised the rod again and stepped toward him, he did so. The driver touched the rim of his cap in my direction before he climbed back in his seat and locked the door. I could see his eyes watching where the man went in the mirror.

It was then that we both looked relieved as Connor returned. He gave instruction to the driver and climbed back inside.

'We are in luck, Maddie. I have tickets for the next sailing. We are going to board, and I will explain once we are on the ferry.'

8

I must admit that the crossing over the water was not something I enjoyed. I had never felt the sensation of a mass of uncontrollable water moving the floor I stood on before. It buffeted me one way and then another before my stomach had come back to centre. I had to stand, feet at hip width apart on the deck, as soundly as I could, where I was able to breathe the cold wet salty air for the short crossing.

'Short crossing,' I mouthed to Connor, as that was what he had assured me it would be; but to me every bump, dip and swirl the waves made added to my overall discomfort. There were people also suffering inside the shelter of the cabin — some were in a worse state than I — but here I stood leaning against Connor for shelter as I watched the land of my birth disappearing from view and looked up at him.

For his part, he was like an old sea dog, not fussed at all. He was smiling at me as usual. He seemed to do a lot of that. It made me wonder if he was just happy by nature, or if it was my ignorance of the outside world that made him think I was so amusing. Although it did not feel like he was laughing at me, there seemed no menace in the man. That was one thing I liked about Connor: his lack of malicious spirit. He was so gentle. I had to look back at the water, for it must be affecting my brain. I had known this man a day, and here I was admiring his character as if I could truly know it. Ma would say that you never knew a man's temper until the brew was in him or his luck with money was out. Then his true nature came through.

'So what humours you now?' I asked, but I was already looking out to sea and toward England. My future lay with another man, who I was certain waited for me on the next piece of dry land we had the pleasure of standing on. I suddenly realised that if we did in fact find Samuel, then this might be the last time I looked back on Ireland. The thought occurred to me as if the mist swept the notion through me. What a strange feeling. I shivered involuntarily. I can't say it was homesickness, but it certainly caught me unawares. I steadied myself against Connor's strong and steadfast frame. His feet were planted more firmly than mine on this sheltered part of the deck just outside the cover of the cabins. He was my anchor, my rock in a tumultuous sea, and I needed him. I only hoped that when we reached land again, I would remember how to think and act on my own, for there was no room in my future for him.

'You're cold. We should go inside. Don't want you catching your death, do we?' he said, and held my shoulders in his gloved hands.

'No, I prefer being out here. People are not looking very well inside.' I swallowed, hoping he would not realise how near to joining them I was.

'Fine,' he said, and wrapped his arms around me. 'In answer to your question, I was just enjoying the moment.' He breathed deeply. 'I love the fresh air and the space you find when you're at sea.'

'Aye, well I'm all at sea at the moment. But without you, Connor, things would have been so much worse for me. I owe you,' I said, and glanced shyly up at him.

'You owe me nothing, lass. You're good for my soul.'

He squeezed my shoulder reassuringly, and we stood there for what seemed an age, both enjoying the moments that passed by; he standing firm to my back, offering warmth, comfort, security and feelings that I can only describe as giving pure joy.

Oh, Connor, you are like a guardian angel, I thought, but did not say the words. If Ma could see me now! I stifled a laugh.

How I would explain my journey with Connor to Samuel I did not know, but somehow I would. He was my friend — that was it. He was related to our village priest and he was just a caring friend. That should do it. After all, the man should be grateful of Connor's help in getting me there. A fine mess I had made of it on me own.

Eventually, we saw the distinctive outline of Liverpool appear. I had heard about the two dominant towers of the Royal Liver Building, but nothing had prepared me for their grandeur or their size. 'Look at it!' I squealed. I knew that this port was and had been a busy place for centuries, never so as when my own family's ancestors escaped this way decades before; but I felt small amongst its scale and business both on the water and off.

Connor pointed to the buildings either side of the towers. 'They're all splendid, aren't they? There's a Port of Liverpool building and one . . . ah, I forget its name. This place has been a hub of trade for centuries. See over there, that one with the conveyor thing coming up from its bowels? That's a banana boat.' He shook his head. 'They come all that way from the hot countries, and then once they arrive they take days to unload. Still, enough chatter. Come; we must be ready to disembark, for this will be a busy port like none other you've ever seen before,' he said, and tugged my hand.

'I have only seen one before, and that was from inside an automobile,' I reminded him. Everyone seemed to have forgotten their feelings of sickness and quickly rose to sort out their belongings.

I fell into step behind Connor and held his hand as we jostled past people without any luggage at all. I saw the steerage passengers further down the vessel, dressed no better than I had been just a day or so ago. How long that seemed to be, yet it was no more than that. I felt so at home in my new clothes.

The number of vessels docked or docking surprised me. The air was not fresh, as it had been out at sea, and the noise had changed from crashing waves and seagull's kwaarking to shouts of men, the calls of birds drowned out by the noise of machinery. The chatter of people provided a constant background hum. It was becoming overpowering and almost overbearing. There were goods ships, ferries, and what I supposed to be a great liner from across the ocean. On land you could hear the noise of haulage from cranes, trains, drays and large vans. But I had not realised how much my grip on Connor's hand had tightened with every step we took as if I would never release him again. When we found our place in the disembarkation queue, he looked at me with a quizzical expression. 'Where's that confident young woman who gainfully strode out of my house this morning?'

I had to swallow and force a smile, because I had no idea. 'I'm here,' I said.

'Good, because you need her, and it would help me if my hand was still useable by the time I reached shore. I depend on it.' He laughed as I instantly let it go.

He placed his arm protectively around

my shoulders. 'Maddie . . . Maddie . . . ' he muttered under his breath as much to his thoughts and not really to me at all.

It seemed an age before we were safely down the gangplank, through the crowds onto a train, and then in the city itself, standing case in hand staring at the huge neoclassical building of St George's Hall in the distance. It all seemed too much for me. The pace of everything was so fast. There were more people and motion here than anywhere I had known, and my anxiety was heightening. I was in a land built for giants, and I felt small. I'd only been used to single-storey cottages and a solitary church with a spire. Buses, trains and trams and automobiles and horse and carts . . . so many ways to travel that it all amazed me. If this was what England was like in the 1930s, what would the vast and beautiful land of the Straits be like? Would it be as the poetic descriptions that Samuel had written to me about, or were the vibrant colours pure figments of his imagination and the reality as noisy and damp as the day was here? I suddenly felt like I had lived in a bygone era, one that was threatened by this new faster world. If I tried to warn Ma and Pa what the future held, they'd not listen to my 'fanciful' notions.

I swallowed and realised that Connor was talking to me. 'Mairead!'

The use of my God-given name made me snap back to my senses. 'I'm sorry, Connor. Could we perhaps get a cup of tea and a bite to eat somewhere first?' I asked. I suddenly felt quite light-headed.

He looked at me and laughed. 'Turn around,' he said, and spun me so that I could see clearly the tea rooms behind me. It was all I could do not to keep spinning. I realised the motion of the deck was somehow still in my legs.

'Oh!' I said, and laughed as he opened the door for me to enter. I swallowed as I was greeted by warmth and the smell of tea and coffee on the brew.

The city outside this little haven looked as though it was full to bursting point. There was so much wealth — I could see it in these buildings and some of the people; but I saw poverty here, and tenements too. Would London be the same? What about all those places that people like my great-uncle Kenny heard about who travelled across the oceans to the Americas? Had he found a good life there, with colour and food aplenty, or more tenements? We'd never heard of him again. That side of the family hadn't done so well in the hard times of famine. So many family bonds were broken and lives lost. Yet, here, wasn't I just following another dream? I looked at Connor. He was real, and so were my clothes and this tea room. I sat down on the chair at the small round table with its white linen cloth on top of it. It seemed as if they could not build homes quickly enough in this place for the many, but the few had a very privileged life, like this. The waitress appeared in her black dress only broken by a starched apron.

She looked at me and I stared back at her. Her hair was neatly pinned in a halo-like plait around her head. By contrast, the other waitresses had short neck-length hair that was somehow crimped in place. I wondered if I too should cut my hair off and become a modern woman like some of those seated at the tables with fur collars to their deeply coloured coats. True, there were a few more normal folk about, enjoying a cup of tea as a treat or a pastry; but the quality of everything in the place, from brass lamps, silver cutlery, fine porcelain and the uniform of the serving women, all dripped of affluence.

'Tea, jam and scones for two, with egg sandwiches, thanks,' Connor ordered politely.

I realised that I had been expected to say something, but I wouldn't have known what to order. I doubt they did warmed soda bread or Guinness cake here anyway.

'Yes, sir,' she replied, and smiled at him coyly.

I watched as she actually dipped him a little curtsey before leaving. 'Why did she do that?' I asked, and watched her walk away between the tables. I swore she was glancing back at him.

'She would like a tip when we've done,' he said, and smiled beguilingly at me.

'I could give her one, to stop flirting with the customers,' I said, and he stifled a laugh with his hand.

'If I did not know better, I would say that you are being protective of me,' he said, and sat back in the chair and looked me straight. I met his eyes, and could plainly see how much he was enjoying my reaction.

'I just don't think it projects the right image. It's a bit grovelly,' I replied.

'If she flirted with the customers, she could lose her job. It is not that kind of establishment,' he said, placing his hat on his lap.

'Can I take that for you, sir?' She had returned with china cups and plates balanced upon her arm. I watched, admiring the skill and ease with which she transferred her load to the table. She then took his hat and coat. She tried to take mine, but I refused to relinquish them.

'I'd have smashed the lot,' I said quietly. 'I would use a tray. It's like she's showing off.'

He grinned, and our fairy-fingered waitress was back with silver cutlery and jam and butter on separate dishes. Soon she had organised our table so that it had carefully positioned dishes for our food. The scones were warm and crumbly, and the sandwiches melted in the mouth. No crust, which disappointed, but they were pretty.

'Where are we to go to next?' I asked, feeling the warmth of the tea and the fullness of my stomach after the food. I almost felt sleepy. The place was cosy and the day outside grey. I was in no hurry to leave the peace and warmth of the place. Besides, I loved the tea and the little jug of milk. I liked the pattern on the handle of the spoon and the fork that was small and made just for cakes.

Connor leaned forward. His hand found mine as it rested on the table. He touched the back of it with his finger. It was one that was quite rough and not that of a pampered gentleman. His knuckles looked as though they had had a scar running near one of them that I had not seen before.

'The agent's offices are just a block away. From there we will find out if Mr Samuel Blackman is here or if the blackguard has departed without you. Or if he really exists at all, other than as a manifestation of someone's overzealous imagination.'

'Not mine!' I snapped defensively.

'No, not yours,' he agreed.

'Yes, of course,' I said, and fixed a smile upon my face, for I felt no eagerness or rush of excitement to find out, which concerned me.

Connor paid, and with some reluctance we were stepping back into the cold air. I adjusted my gloves, and as he carried my case, we had only walked about ten paces when a man came up to Connor and pushed him back a step with the flat of his hand on his chest.

Connor braced himself straight away and pulled me behind him. I grabbed the case that he had discarded, his fists made ready for the man should he attack again.

'You have a death wish, man,' Connor shouted. I noticed that he had balled both fists as he stepped forward again to meet the man square on.

'Holy mother! Conn, you don't even recognise me!' the man growled. He was a monster of a man: broader and taller and rounder than Connor, his eyes hard as the keel of an iron ship. His nose was a funny shape, and his forehead had a scar running from above his eyebrow to his receding hair line. He stood a foot taller than Connor at least, but that did not seem to bother him at all.

'Deaglan Blaine!' Connor said in a surprised tone. 'How could I ever forget your ugly face?' Connor smiled, but I noticed that he was not as relaxed as he had been. His fists were still balled.

'Aye, yer blatherskite! Since you

helped to contribute to it. You're a brave man coming back here. Have you got fed up of living in that dank swamp across the water?'

'No, Deaglan; the beauty of the emerald isle has not been lost on me. I'm helping a friend, that's all,' Connor said, but did not make any attempt to introduce me.

'If the Kells catch you, you'll be calling me the pretty one when they've done with you.' He looked past Connor to me. 'Got yourself a skirt at last.' The man's manner was coarse.

'Mind your tongue, Deaglan. This lady had lost her way,' he explained.

'Aye, she must have if it's your company she's keeping. Or does she like a man with a pretty face and the punch of the devil?' He stared down at me and I looked back, but I was frightened of the brute and I think he sensed it. His lip curled up at one side.

'Where are the Kells?' Connor asked. I had noticed him glancing around as if they too might pop out of a side alley and knock him backwards or over. 'I thought they'd gone down the smoke for the Williams and Skink fight?' Connor snapped his words out, and I watched a nerve twitch by the side of his eye. I had stepped to the side of these two men. If Connor was going to be attacked, this brute would feel the full force of my case on his ugly head. But their conversation made me realise where Connor's wealth had come from. He was a fighter. A good one, for sure. For his nose still ran its true course.

'Aye, they are, but they are back tomorrow, and if you are in this city they'll find you. They raised you up to dizzy heights, but you was supposed to stay until you were all wrung out, not stop when you were at the top.' Deaglan's words explained my friend's wealth and his clash with his 'calling' and his family's disapproval.

'That's my decision to make,' Connor said, and his fists unclenched.

'No, lad; you sold your soul to the Kells, and in their book that means they own you till they say you have no more value. Get it?' Deaglan leaned forwards. 'You seem to think you can outrun them, but they don't forget. That strip of water will be no more than a stream when they decide to make atonement. They'll step over it, show you the error of your ways, and step back.'

'No, that'll not happen, and I don't think they'll find me that easily. Now, pleasant as this is, I must be on my way. You never saw me,' Connor told him.

Deaglan nodded. 'Very well. But do not go near any of the clubs. Just row back to the peat bog, and I'll not say anything unless someone saw us; then I'll sing like a birdy. Bye, miss,' he said, and looked at me. 'Enjoy him whilst he still has life in his veins, and his little face is all pretty still.' The obnoxious man blew me a kiss and then walked off.

'Damnation! What were the chances of that, Maddie?' He was still staring after Deaglan. 'Some ghosts haunt the living.'

'He's no ghost; but you have enemies, Connor. And what he said about them going to Dublin to find you is true, isn't it?'

He turned his troubled eyes to me. 'Aye. I only returned to try and convince my sister and parents to come with me to Boston. I wanted to make a new start for us all, but they refused. Told me my money was tainted and my soul damaged. I risked being caught for them, and they would see that as just retribution for turning their chosen path for me down.' He shook his head.

'Yet you came back here for me?'

'Not only you. You see, I still aim to leave. It is just that our paths were both going to Liverpool, so why not?' He shrugged his shoulders.

'We best get you off the street, Connor,' I said, and this time it was me who led him by the hand, realising for the first time just how powerful those hands were.

9

We found the doorway quickly enough that had the agent's name written clearly alongside the third buzzer down. Giles, Magdalene and Simms — the names as bold as brass; the brass they were engraved upon, that was. I pressed the button and waited.

'Now or never,' I muttered.

My usually attentive Connor was looking behind us as if we might be stalked. The brim of his fedora was tilted slightly downwards, which made him look even more handsome, but I knew it was not for that reason. My hero was trying to blend in so that no one else recognised him.

The buzzing sound that the doorbell made took my attention. The door opened, and a prim-suited lady with pale skin, yet high colour, stood before us. She had a fine tweed suit on that was smart, practical and well-used. I took a guess that she might be four or five years older than me; but with her face made up and her hair neatly coiffed, she had the bearing of one more senior, or perhaps cultured.

'You may enter.' She pronounced her words not in the local accent that was quite distinctive, but in perfect cut-glass English, or so it sounded to my Irish ears. We both followed her inside. I suspected that Connor was keener than I to follow her up the steep narrow stairs. I could see she was thin, and the reason why. If every time the bell buzzed she had to come down, then she would be as fit as a fiddle and skinny as a rake. Sayings tripped off my mind's tongue as I entertained every thought but the one I was there for.

Connor placed a guiding hand on my back when we reached the third landing, and I stopped before following her inside. Two days previous, I would have thought her the picture-book model of fashion. Now, dressed as fine as I was, her apparel looked smarter than my old clothes, but not a patch on the ones I wore comfortably today. How quickly things change.

'Go on,' Connor whispered.

I went ahead. The lady was now seated behind an old wooden desk just outside another glass door, which shut off an office where we could see the figures of men talking, writing, speaking on the telephone and laughing. One was smoking a cigar or somesuch. Outside, screened off, was this solitary woman — prim and proper, not a part of their world at all, or so it seemed.

'What can I do for you?' she asked, and looked straight at Connor with a polite smile on her immaculately made-up face. Her horn-rimmed glasses gave her a schoolmarmish appearance.

'We are trying to trace a Mr Samuel Blackman,' I said. It was my adventure after all, so I decided that I needed to speak up, or go unseen and ignored, and I had had enough of that in my life.

Connor nodded. 'We understand that he is to depart for a position in the

Settlement Straits, and we were hoping to meet up with him before he departs.' He looked pleased with himself as he spoke.

'I was hoping he might have left a message for me,' I added.

She glanced up at me and raised one eyebrow. 'You are?'

'Miss Mairead Mulligan,' I said flatly.

'If you wouldn't mind checking for us, we would be so grateful.' Connor took off his hat and smiled at her. Her starchy manner softened.

'S. Blackman.' She repeated the name as she stepped over to a high cabinet, and when she opened the drawer, I could see it was filled with buff paper files. Her delicate fingers almost ran across the first few until she pulled one out. Opening it, she read the paper inside before straightening her skirt and sitting back down. 'Yes, he is to be an assistant planter at one of the Johor Bahru rubber plantations, Malaya. Due to sail in three days.' She looked pleased with herself for remembering where his file was.

I felt a rush of emotion run through me. I would like to say that it was pure excitement, but that seemed to be more what Connor was showing.

'I'm Miss Perkins,' she said to him, and smiled.

'Pleased to meet you, Miss Perkins. Is there anything within that file that might reveal where we could contact him?' he asked.

'I have a letter here for a Miss Mulligan, should she appear in time before his sailing . . . ' She looked up at me as my hand shot out for it. Perhaps I was not dealing with this situation as smoothly as I should, but this was all so new to me.

'That's me!' I exclaimed. I sounded a tad neurotic even to my own ears. Connor grinned and Miss Perkins looked at me, obviously unimpressed.

'Can you prove it?' was her stark reply.

'Yes; I have a letter addressed to me from Mr Blackman.' I had kept the letter in my pocket in case it was needed. Although I was sure it had been written by Peggy or Ma to send me back to them again, I was still loath to part with it. I showed her the address on the letter. In my rush, I had forgotten that this example was charred. 'I have a certificate of birth too,' I added, suddenly remembering that of course official proof was needed.

'Perhaps that might have escaped the fire intact,' she quipped, casting a knowing look up at Connor.

I could have snapped at her, but Connor was smiling back at her jest. I had to open my case on the floor and remove the purse where I had kept my papers safely. I closed it and showed her my document.

'Here you are, then. I hope you find him . . . well,' she said, and stood up to open the door for us. Our business was apparently over.

'Do you know where he is staying, Miss Perkins?' Connor asked as he held the door open.

'I would have no idea, but perhaps the letter will inform you.' She smiled and sat back down at her desk to continue her work. Apparently we could show ourselves out.

'One last little detail, Miss Perkins,' Connor added as he replaced his hat at a jaunty angle. 'Have you any idea how old the gentleman is, so we may look out for him? You see, we have only corresponded with him and have not actually met.'

'Yes, I can tell you that. Let me see . . . born 1901. He's 31 years old.'

'Thank you,' Connor said. 'You've been very helpful.'

Back down in the hallway, neither of us were keen to go outside to read the letter. So I stopped and opened the envelope in the shelter of the hallway.

'Tirty One!' I said.

'Or as the English say, 'Thirty One!'' he said, and laughed. 'He's a little more mature than you, Maddie, but he is hardly old.' Connor looked at the letter in my hand. I held it so he could see it too. We had come this far together in my quest; I could hardly cut him out now.

This letter was brief.

Dear Mairead,

I hope you manage to make the journey in time and without incident. I was concerned that you had changed your mind when my last letter did not receive a reply. However, I expect that you will make every effort to fulfil our arrangement, as I changed my original idea of having a companion with me for one of taking a wife there. I hope I have not wasted my time.

You should make haste to the Ambassador Hotel forthwith, bringing your birth certificate and passport if you have one. If not, then we have more paperwork to fill in, and the sooner you are my wife the better.

Regards,
Samuel Blackman

'Not a poetic sort then, like you had described.' Connor looked at me and grimaced.

'Why would I possess a passport?' I said in dismay. 'He must be panicking, as it must appear to him that I have deserted him and foregone my part of the bargain.'

'You wouldn't need such documents, so he can hardly expect you to provide one. It sounds as though he has thought of that one anyway; and as his wife, you might be able to be on his paperwork.' Connor opened the door to the street, giving more than a cursory glance outside. 'I'm no expert on these matters, but he is such a worldly man, I am sure he has his plans in order.'

I was silent, and left it to Connor to steer me and my suitcase along the broad street and down towards the hotel, which was fortunately near enough to walk the distance within a quarter of an hour.

'I don't know what to say, Connor. This note is so businesslike . . . and cold.' I looked at him as the lost bairn I felt like.

'Yes, it is businesslike, and masks hurt or concern; and it was left at his offices, so he would hardly write a lover's note, would he, with Miss Perkins looking after it,' he replied; but his eyes scanned the foyer of the hotel as we entered. The entrance was grand; its tiled floors, black and white, were quite striking. Above, a huge chandelier hung from the high plastered ceiling. Vast green leafy planters stood beside marble columns; a big sweeping reception desk opposite was polished in a dark wood with brass edgings. Stairs that must lead up to the rooms swept away up and out of sight, with a deep rich patterned carpet.

'I don't know about this.' I shook my head. 'Will they let me in?'

'Yes, you do. They will, you are dressed as a lady, not a maid!' he replied, and hooked my arm in his strong hand and walked me, bag and baggage, towards the receptionist.

'Mr Samuel Blackman's room number, please.' His voice was authoritative.

'That would be room 19, first floor. Take the stairs to the right,' was the polite reply. 'Do you need a porter to help with the bag, sir?'

'Thank you kindly,' he said. 'No, I

can manage.' And before I could object further, he began to march me up the stairs and along a corridor, and then we stopped. 'Now, here is your bag. There is the door that leads to your future, just over there. And here, sweet Maddie, is where we must part.' Connor's eyes looked sad, but his manner was determined, almost urgent.

'You're leaving me so soon?' My voice almost rose in panic.

He cocked his head on one side. 'You cannot think he would take kindly to you turning up with a prize fighter in tow, would you?'

'But what if he is not a gentleman, like you? I mean, what if . . . ' I knew what I wanted to say, but the words sounded so feeble.

He sighed. 'I will be in the bar, waiting for you with my oh-so-hunted head, hiding behind a newspaper. Find me, or have a boy fetch me, if all is not well. I'll hang around for an hour, but no longer than that. I should've realised that the Kells would not have taken my resignation with good grace. I have a ferry to catch.'

'You are very kind, Connor.' I smiled at him. I never thought that I could become so attached to someone so easily, and I feared that I had inadvertently placed him in danger, yet I could not find it in my heart to tell him to go now. I needed that hour.

'I know . . . now go.' He waved me off and ran back down the stairs two at a time. It was 2:30. By 3:30 I had to decide my future.

I knocked on the door of number 19 and waited.

10

'Come in!' the voice snapped.

I slowly entered the spacious room. The double bed was not as grand as Connor's, but more modern, with a cream quilt cover thrown casually back. The man who rose from the small desk by the window was in his shirt sleeves. His braces covered a slim chest. He had a drink of what looked like whiskey in one hand and a cigarette in the other. He put the butt of the cigarette out by stubbing it in the ashtray with all the other butts. I stifled the urge to cough, as the air smelt heavily of smoke. I was used to the open air, and this room was stuffy. He then took a swig from the glass before placing it down on the table by his papers.

I had only taken a solitary step inside and placed the suitcase down on the floor. 'Mr Blackman?' I asked.

'I thought you were my lunch arriving. Who are you?' His hair was as dark as Connor's was fair.

'Samuel . . . ' I wanted him to realise who it was he was greeting. I braced myself for a hug or outpouring of emotion.

'My God! You are the Mulligan lass!' he said, and smiled — almost laughing, I thought. His eyes were dark, not as easy to read as Connor's were. He was good-looking, and thinner than Connor; in a way rougher in his dress and manner, which seemed odd, as it was Connor who was the fighter and Samuel who was the 'gentleman'.

He walked past me and shut the door, then placed his hands on his hips and looked me up and down as he came around in front of me. 'I thought you were a simple peasant lass, yet you turn up looking like a . . . '

'I beg your pardon?' I said. I did not like his tone. 'Like a what?' I lifted my chin so that I could stare straight into those dark pools defiantly.

'Sorry, Mads. You must excuse my direct manner, but I say as I find,' he explained.

'Do you always judge people so quickly?' I asked, still not sure what he thought I looked like.

'I am an astute judge of character, Mads. Here, take off your coat and let's have a proper look at you,' he said as he drew the curtain wider to let more light into the room.

'What?' I was confounded. He had not even asked me how my journey was and what had happened along the way. Was I hungry, thirsty? He asked me nothing.

'No need to be shy. We'll be married by special licence and off in a few days, so take off your coat and I'll tell you what we need to do.' He stood looking at me with his arms folded across his chest. I noticed the stain on the fingers of his smoking hand.

'Peasant stock!' I snapped. 'And what is it that I am looking like, exactly?'

He dropped his hands to his sides.

'Very well, we shall get this out of the way and then sort things. I was expecting a simple wench who wants to better her lot, but who has had few opportunities in life to. One who knew when not to answer back and ask stupid questions. From what you've told me, you're healthy, strong, and have some education and intelligence. All qualities you will need, to adjust to life out in the East. You showed enthusiasm for travel, so I decided that I may as well take an able wife with me and save time looking out there. One who realised that here there is a big shortage of eligible men thanks to the war. You can learn the rest of your duties as we adjust to our new life. Mother was a lot happier about me going, knowing I would have a woman to take care of domestic things, and I clearly could see there would be benefits.' He winked at me. 'So off with that coat and let's be having a look at you,' he said. He undid the button that was holding it closed over my suit. It slipped off. Instead of looking at me, he was feeling the cloth and lining. 'Where did you get this?' he asked before dropping it on the floor.

'It was a gift.' I could not think what else to say. I had never thought how difficult it would be to explain my good fortune of the past day and night.

'From whom?' he asked, and his eyes darkened further.

'A friend,' I said quietly.

'You have such friends?' He cupped my chin in his hands, and his cigarette and whisky filled breath was on my face. I didn't like this. I didn't like him. But I froze. I had accepted riches from a strange man and could never explain the reason for it unless I introduced Connor to him.

'Only one, and I wanted to look nice for you.' My words sounded pathetic even to my own ears.

'Only one, eh?' he said and before I could respond he clamped one hand behind my head and forced his mouth onto mine. I pushed him away, but despite my shoves he continued to kiss me with such force and passion that when he stepped back, I had to gasp for air. 'Is that what you do to get your finery?' He shook his head. 'I can see you like it. Very well, the journey will not be as dull as I expected. You can be a 'respectable wife' now.'

'How dare you!' I said and grabbed my lovely discarded coat from the floor.

'I dare, very well. I had thought to give you a chance at a new life, Mads, but it looks like you are no stranger to accepting a hand up from the peat bog of your birth. No matter . . . ' He scratched the back of his head.

'No matter!' My ears were ringing with his insults, my mind a whirl with words that my ma would have fainted at if she heard me express them.

'You will have to have a thorough medical. I'd hoped you would be a maid at least, but where we're going you will have to amend your ways. We shall make a new accord, Mads. You will act as my wife — and do not stray or I will divorce you out there — and we shall carve out our future. I am married to my work. You will have what my salary can provide and a respected place in the society of the colonial clubs. Your children, when they occur, will have maids, and you only have to stay sober and act like a lady. Oh, and we'll work on that accent so that you can speak simple English well. Do you think you can manage that?' He smiled at me as he picked up some papers. 'Once the doctor has checked you over, you sign these and we shall go to sort out the legalities. We'll have two nights in a comfortable bed with good food aplenty, and then, well, we'll just have to make the best of life on board ship.'

I stood there shaking my head.

'Now let's look in here and see what you've brought, for you'll need some new clothes en route or you will swelter.' He reached for my bag, but I grabbed it first. 'Come on, don't be a child. What's yours is mine — or soon will be.'

'No! Nay! Never!' I snapped out. 'I'm

not seeing a doctor. There's nothing wrong with me!'

'Woman, if you've already whored yourself, I want you checked before we go on board a ship together. I cannot be ailing, and I will not take a wife who is not healthy!' He swigged his whiskey.

'You've not a romantic bone in that body of yours, have you?' I remarked as I slipped my coat back over my shoulders.

'No. That surprises you? You who would run off with a man she's not even met. Turning up in the clothes that only a man of money can have bought her, and you accuse me of not being romantic!' he shouted; but he did look hurt, and the guilt that I felt made me swallow hard.

'Samuel, I was near destitute . . . '

'And that is your excuse? Many are, but you had the advantage of beauty to pave your way. I should be honoured you turned up at all. Old, is he?' His words were bitter.

'No, he is younger than you and

more of a gentleman. These were his sister's . . . '

He laughed. 'Is that what he told you? I thought you had sense.'

'It is you who cannot see. I am telling the truth, and if you cannot believe me then there is no hope for us and this venture. I wish you well,' I said, and stepped towards the door.

He had a long stride and easily got there before me. 'We can make this work, if you agree to fulfil your promise. To be honest, you are pretty enough to pass, and that is better than if you arrived looking as if you should have brought the farm with you. Let us begin again.'

I looked up at the clock on the wall. It was ten minutes past three. I had twenty minutes to find the man in the bar who would hopefully stand by me and help me out of this mess.

'No, Samuel! I made a big mistake coming here. I believed your letters and the beauty of what you spoke.'

'I did not lie, Mads. The place is

beautiful. The colours are vibrant, and I can't wait to start a new life there.'

It was Maddie's turn to laugh. 'Oh my, how silly I've been. You are a passionate man and in love, but not with me; with a world that you are going to. With fauna and flora. With the notion of being a white man in a foreign land. Not with the love of a woman. You want a nurse-maid.'

He slipped his hands around my waist and leaned his sharp nose next to mine. 'I need more than that, and you are a woman who can give it. I'm not cruel, Mads. I'll treat you kindly. Your life will be full of challenge and finery. Be a good girl. I'll not ask any more about this.' He flicked my coat collar. 'I'll make an honest woman of you and give you a life that you could never have dreamed of. How romantic is that?'

Before I could tell him how romantic I thought that was, he covered my lips with his again, gently. When I managed to take a step back, he nodded at me.

'Good, now this is what we're going

to do . . . ' He walked back over to the table.

I did not listen to his words or say anything in reply. Instead I turned the handle of the door and ran. I had ten minutes to find Connor.

11

I ran down the hotel stairs, pulling on my coat and carrying my bag. I did not look back. Why would a man be so heartless? He cared nothing for me; for women. As far as Samuel Blackman was concerned, I was only a means to please him. His mother was also pleased! I slowed down before reaching the foyer and breathed deeply.

I took a moment to calm. I gave in to temptation and glanced back up the stairs. People passed by me, but above their heads I saw Samuel. He was leaning over the banister, peering at me with his cigarette in one hand as he looked down. Yes, I thought, he looked down at me in every way he could. With the other hand he casually waved me 'Bye' and walked away. The cad! I was no more to him than dirt under his shoe.

I walked briskly down the rest of the stairs. I had a few minutes to find Connor in the bar. But when I looked back across the reception desk, I could just see over a group who were arriving, a familiar fedora on someone tall's head just leaving the building.

My heart raced. It was nearly twenty minutes to four. I grabbed the case and made straight out of the hotel entrance and onto a busy street. It was as I stepped outside that I saw him getting into the back of a car and being driven away. A new sensation filled my empty heart: fear. He was with two men.

'Do you wish a car, miss?' the hotel man asked, standing by the door. He looked as though he had stepped out from the past in his tall hat and fine uniform, all buttoned up with shiny brass buttons and gold brocade against his navy wool coat.

'Yes, please,' I replied quickly, watching the back of the vehicle Connor was in.

He immediately flagged one over,

and I climbed in. 'Where to?' the man asked.

'Down there.' I pointed after Connor's ride; the doorman shrugged at the driver and gave my instruction.

'You see that vehicle, behind the tram up ahead?' I asked, sitting forward so I could see clearly and follow the progression of Connor's car.

'Yes, miss,' he answered. I could see a smile on his face.

'Please follow it,' I said, keeping my eyes trained upon it.

'No need, miss,' he said, and shrugged at me in his mirror. Our eyes met. His older, wiser and more knowing. 'That is one of the Kell brothers' runners. If your friend is a guest of them, then I know where they're going, and it ain't no place for a lady.' He looked earnestly at me in the same mirror. I realised with horror I was not going to get this man to change his mind. Whoever the Kell brothers were, they obviously ruled this part of the city.

'You don't understand. They have my friend Connor in there, and he has a ferry to catch ... He could be in danger!' I snapped the words out and instantly felt concerned that I might have said too much.

'Would that be Connor Riley, The Fist?' the man asked. Now his eyes were alive with interest.

'Yes,' I said honestly, hoping and praying that I had not condemned Connor further.

'Oh, man, I saw him flatten Deaglan in the second round ... he had it coming, the little sh — ' He coughed. 'Sorry, miss. Look, if it's all well with you, I'll choose not to get directly involved in this matter, as I have a family to support. But I know someone who can help.'

Without another word, he looked out of his window and we moved off at speed. He did a sweep to his right and stopped two blocks down, then ran into a bar. Three flat-capped men rushed out and got into another car and sped off the way we had just been coming.

My driver sat calmly back down in his seat and smiled at me over his shoulder. 'Now, ferry, is it? Well I'll take you there, miss,' he said, and without waiting for me to reply, he continued driving.

'But what of Connor?' I asked. The hopelessness of my situation was burning a hole into my fractured heart.

'You leave the fate of young Connor to his kinsmen. There's no one likes to see the Kells get the better of a talented lad with spirit, especially one born and bred in the shadow of Tara. You go to your ferry and wait for him to come to you.'

'Do I have any choice?' I asked.

'No, and the police will not give you the time of day, so there's no good you goin' blithering to them. You mention Connor Riley, or the Kells, and they'll have you in a cell before you knows that the coat is off your pretty little back. So be a good lass, and wait for your man as I say. Count your blessings that it was me watching his back when you needed a cab.'

'You were watching his back?' I asked, perplexed.

'Just turn of phrase, lass.' He drove me onto the docks, past the crowds, and then stopped near an official building. I had no ticket. 'There you are,' he said.

'I have nothing much to pay you with,' I said, realising once again my impulsive nature had landed me in a tight spot. I thought of offering him something to sell, or a gift for his wife from the things I had been given, if he had one.

'Don't you worry none. Tell that Connor when you see him that Seamus Mallory saved his skin. He owes me . . . ' He winked.

'Thank you,' I said, finding some comfort in his words.

He sped off, and I was left standing amidst the melee on the docks. I had to find out where the ticket office was, and read the large board to see which ferry he might be going on if he turned up. I presumed it would be back to Dublin;

but how was I to know anything for sure anymore? I could not see a scheduled sailing.

I needed to breathe sea air again. I stepped outside and found a bale of cotton that no one seemed to be doing anything with at the side of the building, and rested against it for a moment whilst I gathered my wits together again. I kept my case tucked tightly behind my legs, for I did not want anyone running off with it as Connor had warned me could happen. It was then I remembered. When I parted from Ma, she gave me a small package, and I had put it safe in my bag, but had been so swept along by events that I clean forgot about it. How could I?

I tucked slightly behind the bale and sank into the shadows whilst I rummaged around until I could open the case and pull it free without spilling the rest of the contents on the dockside. Holding this small treasure tightly in my hand as if it were a lucky charm that God had sent me — if God did such things, which I doubted — I decided I had better re-enter the ticketing and waiting hall before opening it up. I almost ran there. Finding a corner in which to be on my own, I tucked my case safe and looked up at the board. There was no mention of a Dublin ferry this night. There was a big ship, but that was going well beyond Ireland. It left in two hours. There were ferries that crossed the river, but none going to Eire till morning as far as I could see.

I swallowed. How would I ever meet up with Connor again?

I stared at a hall half-full of strange people who were either queuing to buy tickets or waiting to go to a new life, or returning after revisiting their old one. I was just one more lost soul amongst many. I considered the package and began tearing the paper open. Whatever I had to face next, it would be better than leaving this place with Mr Samuel Blackman, and could be no worse than returning to my home. My heart ached to see Connor again. He had shown me kindness, and I felt comfortable with him. More than that, I positively ached for him.

Holding this parting gift in my hands, I thought I should feel homesick, but I did not. I felt anger that for the years I had a secret identity that no one had told me about. I loved Pa, with all his faults, and the boys mostly; but Ma had hated me, and now I knew why. She held me responsible for her mistake. How could she? I might not be of Pa's blood, but I was hers. She was heartless, and I was a bastard, and everyone had known that but me.

The brown paper revealed an old envelope that held a letter. It was addressed to my ma, and it was from someone called Annie. The contents were brief.

My dear sister,
I owe you my life. Thank you both for taking Mairead in. Blessedly, she was born early before I grew large. I know you are expecting your first,

and she cannot be a twin to yours, but I must leave her now. She is small and strong. If I leave her at the mercy of the sisters, she would not survive. If I tell Father — I might not! I understand it is a lot for you to take on. You are so generous. If Mother found out, it would break her heart. Please never tell her that she is not your own. I do not deserve her. Edgar loves me, but it was impossible for a man of his rank to marry a widow. An Irish one at that!

God will bless you for this, I know it.

The enclosed pocket watch was Edgar's. He gave it me to see to the bairn, but I could not do that. I fear the Lord's wrath too much. Perhaps life in America will be kinder to me.

God's blessing on you all always!
Annie xx

I gasped. Ma had let me believe that she was my birth mother, fallen or raped — but she had covered for her sister! There was no mention of there being an attack, abuse or force. My real mother and father had loved each other, but neither had wanted me. Had I understood correctly — he had given her a watch to have her get rid of me? I shivered, not from the cold, but from the realisation that I was not wanted. Was this why everything I did, every choice I made, seemed to have skirted disaster? I had begun to think I was lucky or blessed because I had been saved by Connor, saved by the taxi man; yet here I was alone, scared and unwanted again.

I'd never even known Annie existed. The timepiece was solid and looked expensive. On the back there was a London maker's mark. It was a solid silver fob watch. Grandpa had had one, but that was not silver and not made in London. This must be worth quite a bit; how much I could never know nor guess. But why had Ma not sold it and used the money? Pride would be the simple answer. It represented the devil's work, and her sister's sin. Instead, we had been raised poor and she had given these two pieces of my history back to me as a final cut. I realised it was not out of love and generosity, but that she was now finally free of her burden of duty, to release me into the world to fend for myself.

I looked up at the huge clock on the wall. It mocked me as time passed, and I was none the wiser as to where Connor was or if I was even in the right place to find him, or he me. Well I had made my choices, poor as they might be. I had appeared to the man I thought loved me as a 'wanton whore', prepared to sell my soul to cover my back in decent clothes; and then I had lost the man I wanted to be with to thugs — all in the space of two days. How careless was I? I would not jinx myself by calling it ill fate. But I had certainly landed in one heap of a mess, sitting here in my finery, with solid silver in my hand and a letter from my mother — my real mother, who had fled to America. If ever there was a woman in turmoil, I was she.

I looked to the doors in turn, waiting and hoping Connor would appear like a phantom or an angel. I cared not, as long as he was real to me. He would know what to do. I prayed hard, squeezing the cool metal in my hand; and with more sincerity than ever I had before, I asked for Connor to come back to me. I felt safe with him and needed his help, and quickly. Once this hall emptied of people, I would be a woman alone on the docks, dressed up to the nines and with booty worth looting, but with few actual coins to my name that I could readily use. This meant that whatever the ferries were charging to get anywhere, I would have to take great care in my next choices.

I ached with frustration, worry and indecision. I would give it until the big liner left the docks, and then head to a small hotel. If I missed Connor tonight, I would look again for the first ferry across the water tomorrow morning.

Somehow I would find a way back in steerage to Dublin and try retracing my steps, and journeying to his house. I knew the address, the number and road, so all I needed to do was pray he had gone home; or if not, then convince his daily woman when she arrived that I was a friend, arrived a little earlier than expected. If she recognised the clothes on my back, she might even believe me and let me stay — perhaps. She could hardly call me a thief if I walked up to the house wearing his sister's outfit, could she? I put the timepiece away and continued to pray. God had guided me so far; I just hoped he would continue to do so.

12

The hall was emptying as the passengers prepared to board the liner, so I picked up my bag and headed toward the door. It was now well into the evening. I felt lost here. There would not be a safe place to stay anywhere near the docks. I had to get a tram or train and go into the city centre and hope that somewhere would let me have a room for the night that was not an unsavoury place for a single woman to be. What kind of woman was about at this hour on her own, who was not 'unsavoury', as Ma would say? The only hotel I knew about was the temporary home to Mr Samuel Blackman. It was well beyond my means at the moment, but my hand clasped a timepiece that I had no sentimental attachment to. I could have means of my own. If only I could get it valued properly at an auction house and be given a decent price. But a woman on her own was an easy prey for conmen. I knew so little about the world. Things were hard for a lot of people, but collectors collected all the time, didn't they?

'Miss Mulligan?' The voice took me by surprise, but I had definitely heard my name correctly as the man Seamus ran across the pavement to meet me.

'Did you find Connor?' I asked him eagerly as he approached.

'Aye, we did, but you best come with me. You're just a tad conspicuous here.' He gestured for me to go with him.

I hesitated, but had little choice as he grabbed my bag and walked away to his car, knowing full well I would have to follow him. I did, but as the sky turned dark and there was no sign of Connor, I felt more and more uneasy. I ran a couple of steps to catch up with him.

'Tell me where he is . . . please?' I asked, and tried to take the bag from him, but he clung to it until we were nearly at the vehicle. One of the three men who had alighted from the public house earlier stepped out and opened the door wide for me. If ever there was a chance to run, now was it. But where to?

'Where is he?' My voice had risen slightly and was louder even to my ears.

'He is safe. Come, before the bizzies arrive sniffing around,' he snapped.

'Bizzies?' I stood still. What language were they talking?

'God help us!' the voice inside the vehicle said and muttered the words, 'The police!'

'Why didn't you say that, then?' I asked as I got inside, trying to mask how anxious I felt. I really didn't want to explain my ridiculous situation to a strange policeman. It would sound and look bad. In short, there was no respectable explanation for my current circumstances. If I tried to explain that I had run away from home to marry and elope with a stranger and cross an ocean without my Pa's blessing, well, what would any person think? What would I, had it not been my own personal choice? I had hardly rushed into it. Samuel and I had corresponded over the course of a year.

The moment I was in the automobile, the bag was tossed by my feet, the door was slammed shut, and the car coughed into instant action.

The man next to me touched the peak of his cap in a gesture of acknowledgment. 'Fearghal at your service, ma'am.' He smiled, and I could see even in the half-light that he was a heavy smoker.

'Where is Connor, Fearghal?' I repeated the question, my head bursting with worry, annoyed that I was not in charge or control of where I was going.

'He's safe, miss. We took him to Seamus's brother's place. He'll be all right to sail in the morning. We've patched him up good.' He winked at me, but his words were hardly reassuring.

'Why won't he be all right to sail tonight? How big were the patches that were needed?' I asked.

'Well, we got there fast, but not quite

fast enough. He had a bit of trouble trying to get Kell's heavies to see his point of view. But we helped him, and now that they've got the picture, there'll be no more trouble. You can rest assured on that. Oh, and there isn't no ferry going back to Dublin this night, miss.'

It was with relief that we did not travel far, but to the back of what seemed to be a club of some sort. The car drove up a back alley and stopped by a flickering light and a black back door. I had no idea where I was, or with whom, other than Seamus and Fearghal. God help me! I prayed as I glanced at the night sky briefly before being bundled in through the back door of the building. I heard grunts, groans and shouts and nearly turned to flee; but with Seamus ahead of me, Fearghal behind and another of their friends at the doorway, there was nowhere for me to go. So, boldly, I followed up a narrow stairwell which led to another door. Emanating from behind it were strange noises, though I could still hear the beat of my own quickening heart. This door led to what was obviously a boxers' training room. To my relief, these men were voluntarily hitting each other or being hit. With one man either side of me, I was walked around the edge of the place. Six men were grunting and punching in the three rings in the middle. They ignored me, and I was grateful, for I did not want to look at them. Without a word, I was shown into an office. At one side of this room was a bench, and on that bench was seated a quite healthy, but slightly bruised, Connor Riley.

'You're alive! You're here!' I gasped, and ran over to him and flung my arms around his neck.

He laughed, and after a discreet hug back, we separated rather awkwardly. 'Yes, just about. Glad to see you too, Maddie. I understand things did not go so well back at the hotel,' he said, but I felt him wince as he straightened up.

'You're bruised.' I lightly traced the

line of his jaw with my gloved finger. There was a red mark on the jaw line, but he must have dodged the blow, for the full force would have certainly left him with a bad bruise on his face.

'Aye,' said Fearghal, 'they was trying to break that pretty nose of his, but he has a charmed life, does our Connor.' He laughed.

'It won't be a long one, though, unless you get your . . . ' Seamus looked at me and coughed. 'Unless you move yourself out of town quickly. The Kells were coming for you, but they daren't cross onto our turf, so you turning up here was something they could not let pass. That Deaglan's a slimy toad. He let the word out. Don't fret none, though I shall make sure he sees the error of his ways. You two stay here and we'll see to it, and then in the dawn of day we'll have you on the first ferry out in the morning. Come on, Fearghal.' He gestured to his friend as Connor and I were staring at each other in silence.

'We'll send food in,' Fearghal said as he closed the door.

'You didn't find true love, then,' Connor said. It was not a question.

I shook my head. I was too embarrassed to say what a fool I'd been and how near disaster I had come, yet again. 'You risked a lot to help me, Connor,' I said, and watched him shrug, then wince slightly. 'I'm sorry I've caused you so much pain, and now your life is in danger.' I swallowed.

He laughed at me. 'Oh the pain had nothing to do with you, but I had it coming. I kinda broke my word, and that is not done. The thing is, I'd have kept fighting for them; but they wanted me to play dirty, to throw a big fight when I could win it. That I couldn't, or wouldn't do.' He shrugged.

'You are so noble.' I was taken aback by his shocked expression.

'Maddie, that heart of yours is too big and generous. How will you ever survive in this world?' He was shaking his head as he sat back down.

'No you have been . . . ' I stepped towards him. I wanted to hug that head and stop it aching and make him feel better.

'I have been not entirely honest with you, Maddie.' He stood up again and placed his two strong hands on my shoulders. 'You are such an optimist. I hate to be the one to dent that charming spirit of yours in any way.'

I was not sure that I wanted to hear anything that would reduce the heroic image I had of him in my mind and heart.

'You see, I was not at that station and on that train purely by chance. I was there waiting for and expecting you.' His eyes were staring straight into mine as if he was making sure that I understood the gravity of what he was telling me. I did, but I didn't want to.

I stepped back. 'How so?' I thought and replayed the scene in my mind. 'You could not have known that I would be there. I was locked in a . . . ' I did not want to admit that I had been locked in an outhouse and was left there in the cold.

'Yes, you were expected. And if your father had taken a strap to you when his temper was at its height, he would have no doubt ended up in prison for grievous assault. But he didn't, because he went to ask Father Riley for forgiveness for what he wanted to do. He was desperate, as you had the audacity to walk out of the home he had brought you into and thought you owed him your very life to serve as he saw fit. That is why you were expected to help rear his children and see that they were well. Your 'Ma' depended on your youth and hands to do what she did not see fit to.'

'Father Riley — your uncle!' I realised there could be truth in his words, but I did not want to know it. I wanted fate — God — luck — to have played a part in bringing Connor and me together.

He nodded and continued. 'Yes, my uncle. He is devout, and he was in no way in favour of you taking off as you did, with an English at that. But he also has watched you grow from small child to a beautiful woman. He knew his errant nephew had just been disowned by his brother and sister-in-law. He is fond of me; he knows I would no more fit the garb of a priest than I would be able to fly. He and I have always been close and honest with each other. So he saw two black sheep running in the same direction at more or less the same time and thought to align our departures. He talked your pa down with a whiskey or two and gained his agreement. He then left him to sleep it off and went and told your ma what she must do, including passing on the letter from her sister Annie.' He looked at me with puppy-dog eyes that were sincere, but I bit my lip and stared back at him for a moment.

'You knew all this and you said nothing to me.' I kept my voice even.

'I was not so cynical as they. I just wanted you to see this man Blackman for yourself and for you to decide if that was where your future lay. If not, then I would see you right in Dublin, but . . . '

'But then the Kells re-emerged and wanted to rearrange your face!' I snapped the words out as if I was thinking of finishing the job for them, but he did not look at all threatened by me or my outburst of temper, and I was calm even though inside a volcano was building pressure.

'Oh, more than that, my dear Maddie. The moment I clapped eyes on you, part of me was lost and found all at the same time. I wanted you to reject Blackman of your own doing, because I would like to walk out with you. There is something between you and me, and I know you feel it too. To deny it would be the greatest of sins.' His mouth broke into the broadest of smiles and my heart softened again. He was right and he knew it.

My chin dropped. I had not expected such words. He placed the tip of a finger under my jaw and then gently closed my mouth, until his found mine;

13

Two weeks had passed since I spent the night huddled with Connor on that bench. We were exhausted, and were woken early to slip us back to the ferry point with the least chance of being seen. My head had been in turmoil. I was going back to Dublin. My mission had failed; my intended had only 'intended' to marry me as a convenience and skivvy. Yet I returned with a man who I felt at one with. He had his problems, namely two called the Kells, and his parents who had disowned him. But that was no worse than my own. His housekeeper had viewed me with a great deal of suspicion; and although she only came in Monday to Friday, she had found me a room the furthest away from his the house could provide, even offering to move in whilst we sorted out our intentions. An offer Connor had very generously declined, although our 'intentions' were quiet honourable.

'Morning, Maddie,' he greeted me as I entered the breakfast room. I loved the way this house had a room for everything.

'Morning, Connor,' I replied, and he politely kissed me on my cheek before I sat down waiting for my eggs and bacon to be brought. Once they had, and Mrs O'Malley had gone back to the kitchen, coffee having been delivered also, we looked at each other and laughed. She had a suspicious cast to her that doubted we behaved when she was not there.

'Well, we said we would give each other two weeks to think about what we should do next; and I have. Have you?' Connor asked.

'Yes.' I nodded shyly as I bit a piece of lovely fresh toast. I was still easily distracted by these simple luxuries that Connor took for granted.

'You go first,' he said.

I licked a crumb from my lips and saw him almost savouring the gesture as

I smiled at him. I was in no doubt as to what he would like to do next — or myself, for that matter. 'I think I should make an honest man of you,' I admitted, and felt strangely emboldened at the ease with which I declared my intentions.

'You have not made a dishonest one of me yet,' he mocked.

I raised my eyebrows. 'One thing, though — I do not want you to go boxing again.'

'Oh, on that we are agreed,' he said.

'What do you think we should do?' I asked, hoping that we were agreed about my admission also.

'Well, I think we should marry. I think we should travel, as the idea of far-off places appealed to you. This is a beautiful world, and I am a man of some means. I am also a teacher of mathematics, so I have that to fall back on. This is 1932, Maddie, and there is a big world out there, so why not go and explore it for a while? Then we can settle back here when we are tired of foreign places, and have some peace and stability in our lives again.'

I rose from my seat. I wanted to hug him and . . . But he put a hand up. 'First there is someone I would have you meet.' He looked at his fob watch, and I remembered mine. I had given it to him on our return for safekeeping and never mentioned it again.

'Who? Oh, the watch. If you have mine valued, then I come with a dowry, don't I?' My excitement was difficult to contain. I didn't want to meet anyone; I just wanted to plan and pack, and I suppose run away from all my mistakes. Try to start anew, with Connor.

'Be ready in half an hour. The driver will be there then.' He stood up to leave.

'You're not going to tell me, are you?' I said as I stood up.

'Nope.'

He left the room and I went to change. Men could be so infuriating.

We were driven out of the city and to a small village near the hill of Tara, where St Patrick drove away the snakes.

I smiled, wondering where these tales began . . . or were there any snakes in Ireland to begin with? Like the little people, they made for good folklore.

We stopped by a church and I looked at Connor. I wanted to marry, but did not expect it to be this day. I had hoped for time to prepare for my special day.

He took hold of my hand in his. 'Come with me, Maddy.' He stepped out; but as I did and I looked into his eyes, he must have second-guessed my thoughts, for he shook his head. 'We shall marry, my love, but not today,' he said, and winked at me; but something was preventing him from laughing at me like he normally did.

There was another automobile parked further up the verge, and it looked even more impressive than Connor's.

Inside the church it was quite dark; the narrow windows let in what light they could, but the day was damp and overcast. As we walked down the aisle, three figures stood up from the front pew.

The first, who welcomed Connor with open arms, I recognised as his uncle, Father Riley. The next figure, who stepped to the side of the Father so that I could see him plainly, was Pa. The third man was finely dressed, greying around the temples and looking almost emotional as he stared at me.

'Uncle,' Connor said, and gave his hand a firm shake.

'Glad you both made it,' his uncle replied. 'Maddie, what an adventure you have been on.'

'Father, I . . . ' He raised his hand to stop me there. Confession was obviously not needed, and I was staring at my pa. At first he hardly looked at me, but when our eyes met, both were moist.

'For the love of God, Maddie, hug the man before he crumbles!' Father Riley said, and we did, like I was a child again. Pa patted my back, and after a moment and a discreet cough from the Father, we stood apart.

'Now, Maddie, this man you have not met before; but with some clever research and deductions from Connor, we tracked him down, and he would at least see you this one time. Beyond that, it is up to him and you.'

He had my attention, although I still held on to Pa's hand, for he was and always would be my 'Pa'.

'I am Edgar Penn Hamilton. My family owned an estate near to where you were raised.' He cleared his throat before adding, 'I knew your aunt, Miss Annie, very well.'

'You and she were lovers,' I said.

'Remember where you are, Maddie,' Father Riley said.

'In a place of truth,' I said, and felt Pa tug my hand in a silent plea to reel in my words.

'Come, Connor, we have arrangements to make.' Father Riley took his nephew into the vestry and left me with these two men, one my real pa and the other the man who started my process of creation.

'Why did you want to meet me now when you gave my aunt the means to rid herself of me?' I asked, mindful of the words I used.

'I did no such thing. It was a parting gift because she and I could never wed, and she refused my offer of coming to live in London with me.' He breathed in. 'I could refuse the matches made by my father for a few years, as he was quite old; and then, when I was free and had my inheritance, I could choose to wed her. No one need have known from where she came. I could have had her groomed so that . . . ' He stopped his words abruptly as my pa had stiffened. 'She would not, though. I respected her wishes, and she left as a housekeeper with a good family who were emigrating to America. I arranged passage and everything as we stayed in touch. I had no idea that you existed.' He swallowed.

'So what now?' I asked, numbed by this man; by the pain that my aunt must have felt and the sacrifices she made to let this man go.

'Your mother and I are still in

contact. She runs a hotel in Boston. I helped set her up there. Neither of us married in the end, but we have stayed good friends. We were both too selfish, I guess, and liked our freedom. I now have an estate near Wexford.'

I looked at Pa.

'Maddie, Connor has asked me for permission to wed you.' He smiled.

'I hope you gave it,' I said. Connor was such a gentleman, I thought; even for a man with handy fists, he had a soft and honourable heart.

'Yes,' he said, and did something I could not remember him doing before: he kissed my cheek.

Connor had returned and stood leaning against a stone column at the end of the pew, Father Riley at his side.

'Mairead and Connor,' said Mr Hamilton, 'as my present to you both, I would like to host the wedding on the estate with all your family members present. And then, if you wish it, there is a lady who owns a hotel in Boston who would love to have you stay with her a while as part of your honeymoon gift.'

I looked up at Connor, who nodded; but then his head shot around to face Father Riley. 'All our families present!' he repeated.

'Aye, lad, and it took a small miracle to get your mother turned around in her opinion of you, but there it is.'

Connor threw his hat to the floor and swept me clean off my feet.

'Enough, enough!' Father Riley said in a loud voice, but there was no temper in it, just good humour. 'There is a gathering down at the inn. Come, you two outcasts, and rejoin your clans; for if ever there was a union that saved souls, you two are it.'

The three walked out, and Connor slowly let me down so my feet touched the hard stone beneath them. 'Thank you, Connor,' I whispered, and kissed his lips.

'Come on, plenty of time for that. Besides, I had a little help,' he said, and glanced back up the aisle.

I had run away to find love and make a family of my own; and in so doing, had somehow released the love that was already there within my own, but locked away by secrecy and lies. I walked hand in hand with Connor and gave thanks that now, before us, we only had truth to face . . . and a world waiting to be explored.

Books by Valerie Holmes
in the Linford Romance Library:

THE MASTER OF
MONKTON MANOR
THE KINDLY LIGHT
HANNAH OF HARPHAM HALL
PHOEBE'S CHALLENGE
BETRAYAL OF INNOCENCE
AMELIA'S KNIGHT
OBERON'S CHILD
REBECCA'S REVENGE
THE CAPTAIN'S CREEK
MISS GEORGINA'S CURE
CALEB'S FAITH
THE SEABRIGHT SHADOWS
A STRANGER'S LOVE
HEART AND SOUL
BETHANY'S JUSTICE
FELICITY MOON
THE VALIANT FOOL
TABITHA'S TRIALS
THE BAKER'S APPRENTICE
RUTH'S REALITY
LEAP OF FAITH
MOVING ON

MOLLY'S SECRET

CHLOE'S FRIEND

A PHOENIX RISES

ABIGAIL MOOR:
THE DARKEST DAWN

DISCOVERING ELLIE

TRUTH, LOVE AND LIES

SOPHIE'S DREAM

TERESA'S TREASURE

ROSES ARE DEAD

AUGUSTA'S CHARM

A STOLEN HEART

REGAN'S FALL

LAURA'S LEGACY

PARTHENA'S PROMISE

THE HUSBAND AND HEIR

THE ROSE AND THE REBEL

DEAD MAN'S PAIN

FREEDOM'S FLOW

THE ROOT OF ALL EVIL

We do hope that you have enjoyed reading this large print book.

Did you know that all of our titles are available for purchase?

We publish a wide range of high quality large print books including:
Romances, Mysteries, Classics
General Fiction
Non Fiction and Westerns

Special interest titles available in large print are:
The Little Oxford Dictionary
Music Book, Song Book
Hymn Book, Service Book

Also available from us courtesy of Oxford University Press:
Young Readers' Dictionary
(large print edition)
Young Readers' Thesaurus
(large print edition)

For further information or a free brochure, please contact us at:
Ulverscroft Large Print Books Ltd.,
The Green, Bradgate Road, Anstey,
Leicester, LE7 7FU, England.
Tel: (00 44) **0116 236 4325**
Fax: (00 44) **0116 234 0205**

Other titles in the
Linford Romance Library:

THE RIGHT MR WRONG

Pat Posner

When Tiphanie tells her boyfriend Howard she'll have to cancel their holiday to go and help her brother look after their niece and nephew, the consequences are catastrophic. Reeling from the breakup, Tiphanie arrives at her brother's home in a beautiful area close to the salt marshes, anticipating just a little peace and quiet. But any such hopes are dashed thanks to inconvenient feline escapades, a couple of very lively children, and her rather irksome — yet gorgeous — neighbour Kyle . . .

FINDING THEIR WAY

Angela Britnell

Attempting to shake off writer's block, novelist Fran Miller comes to the Cornish village of Tresidder to spend the summer with her long-time best friend, Lucy. She definitely isn't looking for romance, especially after a painful breakup with her last boyfriend — but it finds her nevertheless in the form of Charlie Boscawen, local baker and heartthrob. Soon she is being wooed with the most tempting confections imaginable. But Charlie has problems of his own . . . and what will happen when the summer comes to an end?

FINDING ALICE

Sarah Purdue

Evie Spencer has always lived life cautiously, wary of trusting anyone other than her beloved younger sister Alice, a talented painter who is studying art in Rome. Then Alice suddenly disappears — and Evie, determined to find her, must throw caution to the winds. Inexplicably stymied by the British Embassy, Evie is frustrated and desperate . . . until the mysterious Tom De Santis offers assistance. But there is more to him than meets the eye. Can Evie trust him, and succeed in finding Alice?

DOCTOR'S DESTINY

Phyllis Mallett

Having lost her husband and daughter in a boating accident, Dr Amy Merrill lives with her aunt and uncle and works at the local hospital. Still struggling after three years to put the past behind her, she befriends a young patient, Jane, brought to the hospital with pneumonia. Jane, she discovers, has run away from her rich father's house to search for her lost mother. And when Amy meets the father, handsome Grady Gilmour, her life will never be the same again . . .

BROUGHT TO ACCOUNT

Paula Williams

When Lauren Chapman is 'let go' from her job at a greengrocer's, her boss encourages her to take a position with a local accountancy firm, Northcott and Company. She does so reluctantly — but when the owner of the company is attacked and left for dead in his office, Lauren is the first person to find him. How is her late mother involved in the mystery? And will a budding romance blossom between her and handsome co-worker Conor Maguire — or is he trying to hide his part in the crime?